WAR AND PIECES

'MUDDLING MY WAY THROUGH LIFE'S MYSTERIES'

BEATE DAYEM STAMNESS

ACKNOWLEDGEMENTS

To my beloved and quirky siblings: You are the essential ingredients in this book, salty, sweet and spicy. Godlike creatures in my younger years, mere mortals later. One other 'ingredient' gave me permission to be part of the book. The rest are fictional or buried long ago.

Thanks to those that struggled through my first shitty draft and found the words to not make me cry, and to all the people in my Tuesday class with Dani Burlison: Alex, Bob, Marion, Sue, Tricia, Pat, Hugo, Rugie and Joyce, with special thanks to Roslyn Ball, Linda Reitzell, Joyce Harr and Kelly McClelland for reading and editing.

To our five children, their spouses and kids, with love. Each one of you enriches my life. My special thanks to the following:

My daughter Lin for her last-minute insightful comments.

My granddaughter Miette who read it all and will never look at me the same again.

My little grandson Charles who suddenly towers above me and volunteered to do the cover.

My son Mike Dayem, poet and author, who ignited my fire for prose and for gently pushing me to the finish.
My daughter Jennifer who is cleverly awaiting the coming of the 'final' version of the book.
My grandkids Coco and Luca. A few more years and Mom might let you read my book. I love you all so much it hurts.

And now to my husband and very best friend. What would I do without your never ceasing love and good humor, the fish you catch, the greens you grow, the wine you make and your highly appreciated internet skills!
Let's grow old together.

CONTENTS

BERLIN, GERMANY, NOVEMBER 1943

The woman is riding an old rusty bicycle. Her belly is big and ripe and barely fits between the high handlebars which she grips with a force, it whitens her knuckles. Will she make it to the hospital in time? She can feel the baby's head far down, curious already, as the beginning darkness is swallowing the narrow path through the forest of birch trees.

The woman looks nothing like her bike. She is a pretty blonde with striking blue eyes. Look up into the darkish Berlin sky and you will find a near perfect color match.

She does not hear the deadly silence stalking her.

BIRTH AND BOMBS, NOVEMBER 21 TO 22, 1943

I am stuck in a wee little spot filled with gurgles and expansions of one kind and another, moving to my Mutti's heartbeat in a tighter and tighter embrace till suddenly all hell breaks loose and I burst from her body in one easy contraction right into the mayhem of war. Mutti made it to the hospital in time and is birthing me while bombs are dropping like background music to her screams. The blast's fury shatters windows and hurls shards of glass into the room. A kind nurse catches me just in time and drops me off in the nearest crib before running for her life.

Everybody runs, doctors and nurses and patients, at least the ones that can run, I figure. The others, I don't know; honestly, I don't want to know about their burns and their screams like roasting chestnuts, but people. Ach. And the blood and the guts! Mutti slumps onto her elbow, her face twisted from pain and terror. She steps onto the ground, picks herself up, hurries to the nursery, lifts me out of the closest crib and runs straight to the bunker. Later she sighs 'it's amazing what we are capable of if needed,' and she wonders if it was me, she grabbed in that frightful rush. Of course, I was me, even if I was the wrong one!

She and I are hunkered down in the bunker now while the Royal British Air Force mercilessly bombs the sh** out of Berlin till most of it is burning. The inferno lasts for days and it will take Vati several days of watching the fires before he can bike to town and search for us, who might no longer be. Right now, we see him gaze into the sky, as blue as his wife's eyes. He feels a sorrow greater than any he has ever felt before; for the sullied soul of his country, for his wife and their new child, and God, please may they be alive, and how can they feed another child?

THE SOUTH OF GERMANY JULY 1944

After the assassination attempt on Hitler, he is ready to sacrifice the whole population. He orders the draft of all men: serve or get shot. Employees of the government must evacuate with their families to Breslau (now called Wroclaw in Poland.) Vati realizes the lunacy of sending families to the eastern border to fend off the Russian army. They must get away. The utter chaos offers a chance to do just that. After work he rushes home. They pack in a hurry. Mutti takes silverware, Vati tosses it, he wants the photos and the few items needed to keep alive and warm.

Millions of stars are out to bid us goodbye. The moon, a silvery sliver on the horizon, will soon bring unwanted light. The night is warm but Mutti bundled us into all the clothes we cannot carry. Gernot and Ulla look like little dumplings. Vati carries two-year old Hartmut and a heavy backpack. Ulla holds on to his hand. At four years old, she has a bag slung over her shoulder, a bit heavy for her malnourished body, and her dark brown eyes are wide open with fear and a sense of importance. Mutti carries me over her shoulder and holds a suitcase. Gernot's blond and tightly curled hair is tucked under a wool hat. At five, he carries his own heavy backpack. There's no hand for him to hold.

As we step into the train station, he digs his hand into Mutti's coat, scared to get lost inside this giant beehive of voices, the sounds of whistles, of sirens in the distance, and the chaos of hundreds of agitated people. It is blackout time, an electrifying darkness charged with herculean happenings and a turmoil that wraps me into a dense haze of grey and black whirls with a piece of memory swirling around. At eight months, I know nothing but feel it. The dread, the changes, movement, maybe there was a train? The memory is elusive but the essence intense, haunting.

We made our get away and are now refugees in the South of Germany, a breath away from a Swiss border town. Life is frantic with throngs of people arriving by the minute. Bombs are falling here also, except for those of us directly at the border. On mayor's orders, people leave their lights on at night to look like part of the Swiss town while all other towns are under blackout order. We will be safe; Switzerland does not get bombed. And the allied forces are already in Paris!

Not one of his friends and colleagues survived the long and terrible siege of Breslau. If they tried to escape, they were shot by our own countrymen, succumbed to starvation, were eaten by rats or else were finished off by the Russians. A total of 170,000 human beings.

THE END OF WAR MAY 1, 1945

O ut of the fog of babyhood emerge objects, sounds and thoughts. Slowly they coalesce and reach my mind, and my eyes dive fearlessly into the vastness of a whole tiny room. There are boxes, lots and lots of boxes. Other objects have no name yet, and their vague shapes and shadows remain unseen.

Mutti walks into the room. It's my first glimpse of her as a person with a face, and I feel a thrill. Hers is a loving face, round and smooth with hair that catches the sun, and those eyes! I must have seen her before but never truly did, only knew she was there like the air around me and I smelled her and listened to her soothing voice.

I am standing in my favorite corner behind a door with my baby doll. She used to be Vati's sock. Now his sock has bright red lips.

"Eat," I say as I lift my shirt and put her – hesitantly – on my belly button, the way Mutti did with me not long ago. Or was it higher up? Yes, I think it was but just as I remember, Mutti breaks out in laughter.

"A bit higher, Sunshine," she says, and I deeply feel my first humiliation.

A faint image lingers from atop Vati's shoulders. We watch the French march into town, a motley group of dirty, tired and happy soldiers. The end of WWII has come. Quickly, Vati gets to know them. He is fluent in French and they share stories of the war, their grief and the joy that it's over. They hire him as their translator and invite us to stay with them in a beautiful villa, the Mauser pistol villa. It is a sunny day. I am sitting on the steps of the entry, and a French soldier hands me a piece of chocolate wrapped in gold foil.

One year later, we move to a town near the Lake of Constance. The small provincial town, ignored by bombs for its lack of importance, welcomes us with the scent of summer and the ugliest face I ever saw, like carved into a pumpkin and left to rot in the hot sun. She is a widow and not pleased when she opens her door to the five of us! We'll be the third family squeezed into her small home.

"Like sardines in a can," she mumbles. Such is our warm welcome into our new refugee housing for the next seven years.

4

THE EARLY YEARS

"The water is ready," calls Mutti before dinner. I stick my legs into the little metal bucket and hold on to her leg while she scrubs me. The fire in the wood stove roars, its appetite as ravenous as mine. What magical power it holds over our life. Mutti's quick wash with a rag is finished almost faster than getting dirty and I don't see the point.

"Out of here" she says, hugging me out. Hartmut's legs are already squeezing in. How white his body is, greenish white, almost see through. By the time I take out my last leg and stick out my tongue, Mutti is finished with him also. He has a thing between his legs. I give it a quick touch. It twitches.

A man with dark hair and scary black eyes shares our toilet bowl with us. It has a chain for flushing. He spends hours in there, loves it like other men love beer or chain saws. I am waiting for him to get toilet trained.

"Mutti, he is so pretty. Why is he so gross?"

"He just got back from the war. He is sick and needs help. His eyes are staring at images visible only to him, and he draws them onto the walls." Mutti wipes them down every day because he paints with what he should properly flush down.

"They are trying to find a good home for him, Sunshine. He'll be gone soon."

Until then, I refuse to go in there and start peeing outside or in my pants. And one day, while digging in the dirt in the middle of the road, wearing a blue bibbed outfit with a duck in front, how I remember that day and the duck, my bladder is about to burst. Should I, or shouldn't I? 'Go for it,' says my inner voice, loud and clear, 'go for it.' And I let the warm, comforting stream water my legs, out here in the fresh air, when a face looks right at me.

"Aren't you a bit old for that? And in the middle of the street?"

I am mortified, tightly squeeze my eyes closed and, like a prophet, experience my first revelation: I will never pee in my pants again. And I haven't. I don't even sneeze and pee like Oma did last week when she visited. She called it just a wee little leak but 'wouldn't mind a good cork,' she said, and Mutti did 'tstststs,' shaking her head. Then they giggled.

They say the war is over, but I don't believe it. When my belly aches from wanting more food, when my body seems to feed off my own flesh, when half an apple or a glass of milk is worth talking about; that's when I know that the war is only hiding. What used to be big bombs are now landmines. You can't hide from them in bunkers because they hide from us in forests, in meadows or in the little creek next to our house. Vati warned us and one glorious morning I sneak out to the little creek to see for myself.

"Stop, stop." Vati screams with his special voice and I nearly tumble into the creek from stopping so hard. He comes running, bends down, his heart beating against mine. "When land mines explode, they turn you into pieces," he explains. I see arms and legs flying through the air, kind of like juggling but messy, and it might be painful if they were my own arms that did the flying. I decide to stay away from mines, but close enough to watch from behind someone else.

Don't get me wrong! Life is good. Mutti takes us to pick dandelions for greens, and their roots and nettles for tea, and she tells us stories, sprinkles the words over us all day long like a soft rain. Vati with his little globe paints the world for us. He'll pull me on his lap, Gernot and Ulla and Hartmut on either side of him, and the world opens in magical colors. We scale Mount Everest, float down to the roar of rushing rivers, we meet people of all colors dressed in exotic clothes or barely any. And when they speak with sounds we cannot understand, an unknown feeling is stirring in me like a window cracking open into a far wider world than my own tiny sliver. I can barely breathe from the thrill of it.

"We need to learn about them instead of warring," Vati explains. But my very best moments are when he scratches my neck with his unshaven chin, till I squeal from pleasure.

NUNS, THE MEAN KIND, AND WINTER'S WOES

I n front of our house is an open area. It's where I practice my curtseys on adults, kids and dogs. When priests walk by in their scary black robes and their sour smiles, I don't curtsey. 'Church' is a dirty word.

My brother Hartmut is sick from the church and their nuns, the mean kind. They cared for him while Mutti was sick. They shared no toys and no warm blankets with him, left him hungry and wet because he is not Catholic. I'll make sure to be Catholic when I am sick and with the nuns. I like to be warm. Hartmut might die one day. I don't know when.

"Bloodsuckers, the lot of them" is what Vati calls them. "Look at their full bellies and proper cheeks from all the food." And I look and see it's true. That's where they stuff the extra food that should be mine.

. . .

We have a nice first summer, what's left of it. Then come our winters, too early, too long, and fierce. Like an ice age they stretch into one long cruel winter, hitting us with a fury that takes our breath away. My little brown shoes have more holes than shoe, Ulla has only wooden shoes, and our coats are threadbare. I don't know about Gernot. Maybe he has no coat. But Ulla and I run outside for quick moments of intense wrestling with winter, our noses leaky and snotty. I use my sleeves to wipe when my handkerchief overflows and Mutti wishes I wouldn't. She has much washing to do and often her swollen hands are blue and bleeding from the icy water.

Behind me, frozen in time, the laundry hangs on the line, motionless, ghostly prisoners doing penance in this raw white world.

Back inside, we hope for the heat to work and for the smell of warm food: crucial foreplay to a meager meal, always the same and comforting in its sameness. Potatoes, carrots and cabbage. Always cabbage. In between, we get treated like kings with liver or lentil soup. And we pick more of the same, dandelions and nettles and whatever else we can find in nature. When the heat does not work, the house smells of stale and smelly socks and my bed gets so cold it hurts. Often, when I pee in my bed and it doesn't dry, I sleep on newspapers and cry myself to sleep, or my eyes sink into the wallpaper and I dream inside its green garland with the purple and pink flowers.

On weekend mornings, we have snuggle fests to warm up. Farts are welcomed for their warmth.

. . .

It is Christmas. Mutti made us a tiny theatre out of a shoe box. She lined it with foil and little figures move around on wires. They wear costumes made of shiny foil, silver, gold, red and blue. With these actors, she creates the story of Christmas for us, all in the little box. It's our first and best Christmas with candles clipped to a tree, a bucket of water for safety, and the glow of the candles turns our living room into a fairyland. Life is a dream. I love my life.

ENDLESS SUMMER

Behind our house, a gently rising hill is covered in beautiful wildflowers. I feast my eyes on them and can barely wait to run into this flowery carpet and stick my nose in it. And my teeth. I am hungry and wish I were a cow and could eat until I had enough, or maybe too much! Would there be space inside for too much?

Mutti is calling us to go picnic on the hill and we take off like tumbleweeds and settle at its edge above a tiny brook. I hold still, a flower amongst flowers, filled with tenderness.

Mutti comes huffing behind us with Hartmut, and we surround her. She has the softest earlobes and skin like velvet. She teaches us about plants and insects, how we all work and feast together, even on each other, in harmony. The bees don't sting, and I feel safe. Mutti hands out dark, hard bread with butter, 'Butterbrot' it's called, and we shriek with laughter for such pleasures, for each other and for the heat of the sun, our barelegged legs crusted in the dirty hues of summer. Mutti smiles, sitting amongst us. Her smile is warm but like dessert, so very rare.

A fleeting vision of things to come, with legs equally naked but tangled, smooth one pair, hairy the other, with one sock still dangling on its toe...

Hartmut finds a wild cherry tree. Its branches hang low enough that he, Ulla and I can climb up and eat. When they had enough, they leave while I, like a sloth, stay and stuff my mouth till I barf. So that's what happens. Too much stuffing makes me barf. Else I'd burst, and yet... what a hard choice. I am hungry, I want more. For the next days, I choose slothing, stuffing and barfing until all cherries are gone but my own.

I cherish long lines of shoppers. I also like short lines because they are short. I love that the sun shines every day of my life. When it rains, I see the sun behind it. And again, I curtsey to women and men, kids and dogs.

"You only need to curtsey to adults," Mutti whispers. We are standing in a long food line. She doesn't like it when I stare at people, so now I stare only at those that limp or have the ugly bag hanging from their chin. Mutti calls it polio and goiters, and if I'm lucky there are cleft palates and club feet, and now she hides my face in her skirt because she knows I am staring again. But she can't keep me from listening to them talk about the things I am too young to hear; I take it all in, don't understand but see it in the streets: soldiers returning from the war, crippled and sick of body and 'in their mind,' they say. 'Millions and millions.' I don't know those numbers. They are way big.

The soldiers come from all the countries where we fought the war, and nobody knows what to do with them, where to put them, how to feed them.

I hear the word 'Hitler' a lot. He is the worstest, and I secretly call him a 'Säckelesmetzger.' (butcher of small balls). Gernot got in trouble for saying the word. Would I get in trouble? They call me cute and small, knee high to a duck. I curtsey to our neighbor and try it out on her, very politely. She yells and calls me a bad girl, and Mutti comes flying out of the house. They quickly agree that I was too little to have known. But I did know and feel an awesome new power, getting away with things if I want to.

A neighbor lady who looks like a general, tall, straight, gray haired, kind of like a man but I don't know which part, she invites us to take a real bath in her tub on Saturdays. Hartmut and I go in first. He discovers a source of fiery noise: under water farting. I giggle and try it too, and we have us our first bubble bath. I love how the bubbles bounce and tickle along my back till they come out and burst. Vati is the last to wash, when the water is nice and brown. Afterwards, the adults talk about the war.

"What's a Stalin? And what's a Jew?" I want to know.

'When you are older, Sabinchen,' is what they say. Then they talk about the USA, where the neighbor lady's daughter lives. She is an opera singer, in a land of wild adventures. My heart beats fast. I stare at her photo. She looks beautiful, her black hair surrounding a white oval face and lips red as blood. I imagine her heels to be higher even than her voice. One day I'm sure to meet her.

. . .

But first, life comes crashing down on us. It's in the early afternoon that an ambulance takes Hartmut to a hospital far away.
Mutti and Vati are deeply in grief, a scary grief, a grief that
settles in our walls and pillows and floats in the air we breathe.
Their shoulders sag and they stare like the soldiers when they
come back from the war, and I cry. Mutti picks me up, and in
the warmth of her arms and the smell of her skin life is good.

Hartmut might be dead. He's been gone for so long. Or was it
just a few days? Time is like a train. It stops and speeds up. I
don't know how. When he finally comes home, I stand on top of
our circular staircase and watch him enter in his brown coat,
frayed around the neck and buttons. Ever so slowly he climbs
up, his hair a mop of dark blonde hair, his face like an angel. He
takes one step at a time, looking so very pale and greenish. He
holds on to the banister and looks up. I stare down into his
greyish eyes and our eyes lock. I feel frozen from a deep sorrow.
This moment is etched into my memory and my heart, this
private moment between Hartmut and me.

After a while, life seems back to normal; or is it? Will it ever be?
Any day the ambulance might be back. I play with him more
often now, but then I don't want to. I don't want to always be
nice just because he is sick. And I don't know what to do and
punch him in the arm till both of us are angry and sad, but
Mutti is mad only at me.

7

LIVERWURST

Ulla is almost five years older than I am and she knows things. Before our midday meal, she whispers that some butchers put humans inside their sausages.

"Ha, they wouldn't fit."

"Silly, they cut them into pieces first and grind them up." And for the midday meal we will have liverwurst, such a rare treat. I shudder. How can I eat if I don't even know WHO is in it?

"Will I be a cannibal if I eat it?" I ask Gernot who is ten and even smarter than Ulla who is nine.

"Only if there are people in it!" He walks away laughing. Mutti tells me not to listen to anybody. Then she dips the knife into the liverwurst, spreads some on everybody's slice of bread and scrapes it off again to have some for the next day. And all of us eat with or without a person in it. Maybe it doesn't truly matter when one is hungry.

EGGS AND BUNNIES

L ife hurries up and holds still all at the same time. It's hard to catch enough breath. Mostly it's about food. There is still so little of it. Herr von Itzeblitz of Zizzenhausen started to deliver eggs to us, his name rolling off my tongue like a well-greased roller coaster. This skinny old man, stiff as a lamppost, kisses Mutti's hands. She looks worried they might smell of onions.

I will never forget him nor the drop of snot that always hangs on his nostril. With much grace, he carries both the eggs and the snot into our kitchen straight to Mutti's pot of soup where he deeply breathes in the aromas of potatoes and carrots, while I stare up at his snot, not breathing at all for fear it might drop. Would I still eat the soup? Most likely I have eaten his snot by now, but well cooked, and my belly doesn't mind what or who is in it.

. . .

Today is Sunday. Vati will bike through the countryside to find farmers who are 'real Christians,' and won't mind sharing.

"They have plenty," says Mutti. "The harvest was good!"

Vati doesn't take long before he returns with a wriggly bag. "Look what I got!"

"Can we pet them?" We ask, our hands already tearing into the bunnies with fierce love.

"Gentle! And yes, you can play with them and feed them, but later they will need to feed us." I lick my chops!

We call the girl bunny Elsbeth and the boy bunny Epaminondas, who once was a mighty Greek warrior. They eat, grow, and diligently hump away their days to make us food. And when they have babies, we eat our first bunny meal. Vati thanks them for their meat. I think that's nice. Life is looking rosy and furry.

LIZARDS AND WORMS

I unleash a grandiose new habit. Mutti knitted a green sweater for me and I lick it on top of my left shoulder. It is fuzzy and not really tasty, but the urge increases fast like a fever, dominating my days and my thoughts. After some weeks, my tongue darts onto that shoulder like a lizard's every few moments. My body yearns for yarn or something.

Vati and Mutti pretend not to notice so I won't feel bad. Ulla feels sorry for me. I don't like her pity and stick out my tongue as far as it goes without falling out. For the next few days I want to stop licking my left shoulder, but my tongue has a life of its own. One day, when doing my lizard lick, Gernot stares at me open mouthed the way I stare at polio people or hunchbacks. I know I must stop. After a few more licks it becomes obvious that each lick wants one other to follow. So I do the LAST one ever. Slow and lingering till my shoulder is wet and my tongue dry with green fuzz. Then I turn my head and look straight ahead all day long, biting my lips to keep the lizard in. When the urge overwhelms me, I squeeze my hands around my head to hold it still. By nightfall, I am healed.

That's when the slithering starts. I feel an odd slippery wiggle down in my privates. I check between my legs and see a tiny skinny head growing towards me, long and longer till we are eye to eye. I am birthing a worm. It is smooth, probably a girl. And then there are more.

"Mutti, I have worms."

Ulla and Gernot had worms also, and I am excited to have my very own. Mutti takes me to the doctor who gives me a pill. A large, round and shiny pill like a frog eye, yellow with black, and I gag and can't swallow and want to keep my worm. But the doctor grabs me and shoves it right down my throat. At home, Mutti says,

"It does not look like a frog eye. More like a big drop of sunlight."

I like that thought and learn how to swallow the sun.

THE MARSHALL PLAN APRIL 1948

"The Amis," Vati explains one morning, using the common name for Americans; "the Amis in their great generosity and political savvy asked us for a wish list, and we asked for Korn. Korn means grains like wheat, NOT CORN, and now we get shiploads of corn from the US."

"Shitloads of corn," corrects Mutti. "We don't know what to do with it. Germans have never used corn inside a kitchen."

But Germans want to be grateful and over the next weeks we try to cook and bake with it. Corn bread, cereal, cakes, all more bad than any bad I know. In the end, our grateful pigs get fattened with it, and Germans do like pork. Daily, new shiploads of unknown items fill our empty stores. Shopping turns into adventure.

One day, a mysteriously curved yellow thing hangs on the limb of the large Linden tree where we play ball and jump rope with our friends. We stare at it without a clue what it might be. Vati joins us.

"It is a banana," he explains, picks it off the clothespin he used earlier to attach it to the tree, peels it and lets us all have a taste. I watch my friends stare at him. They wished they had a Vati like mine. Or just any Vati. Most died in the war.

Mutti is joining us, apron around her waist. She picks me up to take me back, cradles me in her arms and smells my neck like I were a little baby. I love her the mostest right after cake. When her long hair tickles my face, I think of God. He is ancient and still has hair like Mutti's. I've seen it on pictures that the priests hand out and in peoples' homes.

"Mutti, who does God's hair?"

"God's hair? I don't think he has his hair done."

"On some pictures, it looks shorter and darker than on others."

"Those are only paintings, Sunshine."

"Then he might have no hair. He might look like Vati." Vati is right behind us.

"All is possible." He is not joking, and I feel the strange awe of God in my own Father, until Mutti laughs and Vati's green eyes fold into spidery lines!

I have so many more questions. If God is almighty, does he have to be Catholic? And who tells HIM that he can't eat meat on Fridays? He must have a wife!

· · ·

The mailman comes bicycling by and interrupts my thoughts. He stops and hands me a small package. The sun is warm, and I sit down upon the five stone steps of the entry, worn by decades of use, and open it with great care. In it is a tiny little suitcase, greyish green, and a card.

Mutti reads 'from the USA.' A present from halfway across the world sent to me.

"How did they hear about me so far away?" I wonder.

"Kind people buy gifts for little kids like you."

Inside I find the prettiest, softest yellow washcloth ever. I smell it, rub it into my face, get lost in its softness but never use it. It is a treasure worthy of a place on an altar. I hide it behind my socks and only take it out to smell and rub for special moments. Thank you, all you very kind people, for the deep joy you brought into my life.

INDEPENDENCE DAY

They are going to take a knife and cut Mutti's belly open. 'It's for my 'pendix,' she says. There'll be blood. Then they'll sew her back together with thread. Will it match her skin? 'Me, they are sending to Oma, my Mutti's Mutti. She should come here instead to do the cutting and sewing. She is a seamstress. She could put a new button on Mutti's belly. But Mutti won't hear of it, even when I promise to tell her stories all day long.

A young man picks me up in a car, and off we go. He drives the car, I drive him mad. I want to look at things, he doesn't. I need to pee, he wants me to wait. And he stinks of stuff! Cigarettes, socks and other nasties. At a busy intersection in the middle of Stuttgart I get out of the car and run away.

The city was heavily bombed. I walk along a world of charcoal, bloc after bloc of twisted ghostly shapes, burned and left to die like soldiers. I can't understand but feel it and am in awe. I walk into the ruins where I huddle in a corner, the strong smell of charcoal lingering and I finally pee, liters and liters, could have saved the building with it. I stare at the black wall of tar rising in front of me, a vicious giant with jagged edges. It dwarfs me into a tiny creature.

I fail to find the beauty that must have been here once. It has its own sad beauty now. Pieces as big as houses are strewn about like pebbles. It seems wrong. There are bad people. Bad, bad people.

A man is watching. He comes closer. "Little girl, don't play here, it's dangerous. Go find your mother, go." He shushes me and I run. And I think, I always do; my head is stuffed with thoughts. Mostly, I think about me. If a ruin smashed me into pieces, what would happen to my thoughts? Where would they go?

I am hungry and need to find Oma. She lives in Degerloch is all I know. I ask a lady who points to the streetcar she is about to enter. I follow closely behind to look like I belong to her. The smell of people's bodies mingles with heavy cigarette smoke. A soldier sits across from me, bent into himself like an almost empty pillowcase, his cheeks as hollow as his eyes. How many people might he have killed? Ulla could never kill. She picks bumblebees off the street and puts them back onto a flower. I miss her.

. . .

It's a long drive up a hill. When the conductor calls 'Degerloch,' I jump off and land right next to a young policeman. His dark hair is slicked back behind his handsome face and his eyes are friendly. I ask him to please take me to my Oma, proud to remember not to go with strangers.

"What's her name?"

"Grandmother."

He takes my hand and we walk to the police station. It is a warm and sunny day and the station is full of men in uniform. They smile and share a buttered pretzel with me, fresh from the bakery, and some milk, and we spend a splendid afternoon together. They do ask a lot of questions like my name.

"Sabine."

"That's a pretty name. Do you have another one?"

"Mutti calls me Sunshine."

"And how old are you?" I tell them five years old.

After many hours Oma picks me up. She seems irritated.

"You shouldn't have done that. You made us worry!"

Next time I'll stay with the police! They are nicer.

THE BREASTSTROKE AND THE PIANO

Back at home, Mutti shows me the big scar reaching across her belly like a zipper. 'It will be easy to get in now' I say, and 'I love the thought' is what she says.

I notice new things. When Vati comes home from work, he hugs her from behind. She bends her head back while stirring the pot. He puts his hands on her front. One of them gets lost between two of her top buttons. Mutti looks all smiley. He makes noises in her neck. Necking noises, and I hold very still. He can find his own hand when he needs it.

Around that time a big piece of furniture arrives.

"My piano," Mutti screams, her face glowing like freshly polished boots; not as dreamy as with Vati's hand in her blouse but wilder with joy.

Like a most revered member of the family, the piano finds the best place in our small crowded living room. Mutti is not waiting one extra second. She sits and starts to play with a fury I did not know lived in her belly. Like hundreds of horses stampeding towards me, stopped at the last minute by the most delicate butterflies. Never in my life have I – never, ever, - wow! No wonder she can whip egg whites into fluffy clouds like a machine. Her fingers fly over the keys, her foot pushes the pedal and her hefty pear-shaped butt slides on the bench from one cheek to the other; she is part of the instrument. They need each other, those two, like bread and butter. How could she have ever lived without it? She was kind of lost, I see that now as she takes us into her very own world of music.

Sometimes she dances for us. She used to dance at the opera house in Stuttgart. When Gernot finds a certain kind of music playing on the radio, he turns it up and Mutti picks up her feet and a bit of her skirt! And Vati's green eyes change into a cat's, wild and moist.

HORMONES AND HITLER

Again, Mutti and Vati look worried and they whisper, and once again, our rooms fill with stealthy, invisible enemies.

"We must try it. He'll die without." I run from my hiding spot where I like to sit and spy.

"Is it Hartmut? Is he dying?" Mutti cries and puts her arms around me. Vati talks about hormones from sheep. Doctors want to try them on Hartmut. It might save his kidneys. He will be the first person they'll test it on.

"Will it help him?"

"We don't know. He'll die without, but might die quicker with it," he says.

Different whispers, equally haunting, have grown deep roots in me. When Vati moans 'ach, why didn't they leave,' I internalize a deep dread, cook it into a toxic potion. New words like 'Nürnberg trials' and 'not enough of the bastards were shot, they sit in the government like before,' heat the potion to the bubbling point. But any questions are futile. 'You will learn soon enough,' is the best they come up with.

I go ask Gernot who is ten and always has an answer.

"Do you know Hitler?"

He looks at me like 'what a little nincompoop.'

"He is dead. I used to call him a bastard and worse. Teachers came to warn Vati and Mutti. 'It is too dangerous and pointless,' they said, and I had to stop."

"Can I say it now?"

"He is dead, I told you!"

"Bastard," I say and feel silly, like a little nincompoop.

14

WHIPS AND DUNGEONS 1949

Do you know the kind of morning when you wake up and know something extraordinary floats in the air, and you have wings when you walk? On such a day Mutti takes me to my first day of school amongst boys with clean knees and girls with droopy ribbons. I can't wait to meet them and tell them things, and I curtsey and shake hands, nearly bursting from such a day, and my mind is as clear as the mirror when I wipe it with my sock.

"You can go now," I tell Mutti.

My teacher's name is Frau Zöhn. Her lips are bright red and I love her, and I love school. Until I need to pee. I follow the flies to a putrid smelling outhouse. Cut up newspaper is hung up on strings and lies on the floor, used and wet and who knows what that stuff is! I gag and go behind the building. Over the next days, more and more kids gather there, soon creating a garden of little white butts of crouching girls, standing boys, and the area turns slippery and lacks any dignity. I bet the teachers have a better place to pee for their big ugly butts!

For those of questionable behavior there is a whip. Frau Zöhn considers me to be one of them. I am respectful and listen to her every word, but bombard her with my own thoughts, that's what gets me whipped. I feel smarter than she is, just haven't learned as much yet.

For the truly incorrigible ones there is a room outside, the 'dungeon,' the size of a large doghouse. Cold concrete walls and floors, windowless with no lights, it is a prison for those, I think, who will turn into bad people one day.

During recess, we walk two by two in a large circle while eating our Butterbrot. Whenever the circle gets too squishy, teachers threaten us back into the proper shape. And that is school, six days a week!

Over the coming weeks, I complain about it at home. The recess circle, the whippings, the catechism and the cross stitch. Vati does not like what he hears, and off he goes to school.

"Sabine does not need to learn the cross stitch, nor does she need lessons in religion." I imagine his finger pointing right at their faces and am grateful to him. May the others learn the intricacies of God and the cross stitch.

And Frau Zöhn starts to turn whippings into conversation. Shortly after, the recess circle gets dissolved into any shape we want. Thanks to Mutti who is the gently persuasive one. I have seen her talk to teachers. They smile at her.

OF BRAINS, OR LACK THEREOF, AND OF BLONDES

I am the best in my class but don't work at it. Soon I consider myself smarter than Ulla and Gernot and very close to Mutti and Vati, even though I barely know how to read. It's a mystery why this is. During a hike along a steep hill Vati warns us.

"You can climb down but don't walk, you'd lose control."

Of course, I didn't lose control. It was the hill's fault and a tree in the way. You can see me down at the bottom, a bloody unconscious mess, my nose burrowed into the bark of the tree.

My brain is an empty space during the next year. No memories, just thoughts. Lots of thoughts, all day long.

There is something about color. I've first noticed when lines were long, and food was sparse, and I stared at people. But I saw without seeing, like eating a cookie and then it's gone, and I don't remember tasting it. But today, maybe I saw somebody staring at Mutti, but I am sure blonde is better than dark. People never say 'what nice brown hair', it's always 'what pretty blonde hair and blue eyes.'

"Mutti, why is blonde better than dark?"

"It's different, not better."

"But it is. Men turn around EVEN after you, unless you wear a hat."

"Sounds like I need a prettier hat."

I ask Vati if he married Mutti for her blondness.

"No," he clears his throat, "I met her while climbing up a snowy mountain. Her hair was well covered. I fell in love with those sparks in her eyes lighting up like firecrackers. Then she took off her hat and coat. I liked that too." He turns to Mutti. "The more I saw, the more I loved you."

"You devil! Handsome and naughty. Watch out for those, Sabine!"

Vati tells me that we are all the same beneath our skin. Millions of people lost their lives because I guess the Nazis didn't know that. I am trying to be sad over such a high number but it's too high. Maybe if twenty were dead, I could see it in my mind and feel their pain.

EMPTY NEST 1952

Mutti is close to tears, Ulla is beaming from ear to ear, showing off the zit on her chin. I am sitting on the floor leaning against our old flowered sofa, bothered to no end by Vati's torn slippers, by the oil he rubs on his hair, by his chair at the head of the table where he always sits with his typewriter. Who will take his place?

He will be going to London to translate the negotiations for reparations to all victims of the holocaust. Ulla will keep him company and Gernot will join them for the summer. They will be gone for a long time. What will happen to us without them? There is barely time to say goodbye.

When they leave, the house is empty and so is my life. No friends I care about. Gernot and Hartmut play chess or they read. The only thing I love is playing Chinese Checkers with Mutti during those long dark evenings. Every evening is long and dark, and we always play, and I always lose. When I get mad, Mutti promises my day will come, fair and square, and then I'll be really proud knowing that I truly beat her.

It seems like years later when they finally come back home. Ulla wears her school uniform.

"I want it, please," and Ulla, nice as ever, hands it over to me. It is light green and white checkered with a belt and buttons down the front. So very simple and perfect, nothing anybody in town has ever seen. It seems to walk on its own hanging all the way to the ground, my tiny figure barely holding it up. I look like a scarecrow but feel like a princess. People smile. Over the next years, this dress shrinks around me until the seams burst and buttons pop.

And that's my only memory of Vati and Ulla before they leave for Paris.

TRAPPED SNAKES AND STUPID ASSES

But this time, I know exactly what it is I miss. Nobody to wake me up in the morning with a bristly unshaven chin, to hug me with strong arms when returning from work. I miss him for Mutti's sake who does plenty of her own missing. With Ulla, it's different. I don't even know how I miss her. It is as if a piece of the house itself had walked away.

I spend more time with Hartmut. He is getting sicker again. This morning, he showed me his big varicose veins on his chest. They seem to be crawling across his greenish purplish chest like trapped snakes. I am sick of his sickness and try to punch it out of him! But he gets mad and I run away crying.

In the evening, Mutti gets her knitting and tells me stories. I love those and the comforting clicking of her needles. Tonight, she tells me about my great grandfather, a witty guy who had a hat factory with over a hundred workers. He was one of the first social democrats and a city council member. He knew all his workers by name and treated them well.

'We help each other,' he would say. 'They made me rich and they deserve to live well also.'

One day, during a council meeting, he yelled that half the city council members were stupid assholes. It made headline news and he needed to apologize. Next day's headline read 'Half the city council members are not stupid assholes.'

I wish I could have met him! She promises to tell me more stories, but then, things happen quickly.

DEATH DECEMBER 1952

E ight days till Christmas. Vati and Ulla are spending the holidays with us. We are about to sit down, salivating at the vision of home-made raviolis. Outside, a dark night looms into the window, a cold, ghoulish intruder. Mutti is about to close the curtains when she hears a faint sound. "Hartmut." White as a sheet she races to our bedroom as if she knew. Then comes her scream, shrill and feverish. "Get an ambulance, hurry."

Gernot runs outside, gets his bike and rushes to the hospital. Vati is with Mutti. Ulla and I stare at the hot raviolis. They will get cold. What a shame. But we can't eat, can barely smell the fragrant scent of basil. Something is different, we feel it. Maybe this time it's for real.

Sirens approach. They stop at the house. Two men are coming up the stairs for him and I move aside. They put Hartmut on a stretcher, go back down the stairs and all three are out of sight. It happens fast, methodical, like that's how it goes after years of dying. But inside this orderly scene lies a chaos waiting to be felt.

Mutti and Vati spend four days at the hospital. They return at night in a trance, not crying but holding it together.

"What does he look like?" I need to know.

Mutti's voice breaks.

"His body...filled with fist size bumps...they're bursting."

Everybody visits except me. How can I watch his body burst into pieces? Mutti puts her arms around me.

"It is very hard to see. Keep him in your heart, he'll know."

I love her for understanding and am very much relieved.

Vati cries at the funeral, seems to crumble under the weight of loss. I've never seen him cry. We sit in a tent against a most persistent drizzle and I watch his grief and snot overflow from his handkerchief onto the dark suit he wears. It leaves silvery tracks the way snails do. They mesmerize me and calm my mind enough to not burst into laughter. My body wants to laugh, and I am ashamed. Mutti would have told me that some people get goose bumps under a hot shower, and some laugh at great sorrow.

I miss you, Hartmut, and grieve for the pain you had and the life you did not have.

On Christmas eve, everything is the same but different. Mutti hides behind her apron and bakes more cookies than ever. Vati puts up a Christmas tree, its scent the only decoration. No one sings. The house becomes a silent coffin. After the New Year, Vati and Ulla leave again.

Over the next weeks I feel relief at his death. It hung about us for so long, forever expected and never quite happening, and he suffered. Relief turns into guilt for feeling relief. But not for long. I come to understand and forgive myself. Hartmut would have. He must have felt relief himself.

19

BAGUETTES AND BATHROOMS, PARIS 1952

Mutti walks me to an old brick building. It smells of ancient yellowed paper, ink, and cleaners. It's where I will take my test to be admitted to a Gymnasium (a nine-year high school). Only a handful of people are in the room. Not a single familiar face. None of my classmates will continue beyond elementary or middle school. I sit down, excited for my first test, and begin at once. It's easy except for a single word problem about live and dead chickens. I answer the way I believe is expected but fill the rest of the paper with comments about how it should have been worded properly to avoid confusion.

I am the first one to leave, knowing that I did well.

It happens a few days later in a store. Mutti talks to two men she calls Professors. I hear them talk and stay out of sight right around the corner, and now the men are laughing out loud.

"Frau Birkholz, your daughter.... funny. ... aced the test and gave us some very good advice. She will do well in life."

I quietly steal away stuffed with the knowledge of how great I am.

The mailman is throwing letters through the mail slot. One has a foreign stamp with the picture of the Eiffel tower. I rush upstairs and hand it to Mutti. She tears it open and reads, a long-forgotten smile forming on her face.

'Come to Paris for the next three months, then we'll spend all summer at the ocean before moving to Bonn, our new capital.'

Feverishly, she begins to pack and get rid of things. It's good for her to toss the old and make space for what's to come.

An overcrowded train takes Mutti and me on the long ride to Paris. Gernot will join us later for the summer at the beach. The train smells of food and well-worn armpits, and the air is hazy from the smoke of cigarettes. When we arrive at the train station we step into the vastness of a different world.

"Vati," I yell, and run toward him. He swoops me up in one gigantic hug. I want to take a bite out of him, this bow legged and balding guy with his happy face. How I've missed him! And the air is filled with a most melodious music, the sounds of French. There are smells, strong, sweet smells of perfume, sometimes wrapped around sour bodies and mixed with the black acrid smoke of trains. Women wear makeup. I feel happy and strangely at home in this foreign country.

A taxi takes us to our hotel close to the Champs-Élysées. Ulla is joining us, radiant and, at nearly fifteen, with newly acquired curves. We hug and I bump into her breasts and we laugh, then hug again. Mutti is not sure the sheets are freshly laundered, but we don't mind! Outside, we sit down under a large green parasol to see and be seen, like being on stage. It suits me. Vati orders hors d'oeuvres, and the waiter starts us with artichokes which we dip in olive oil and eat with fresh baguettes and a French smile. With my new big wheeled red scooter, I zoom down the Champs-Élysées hundreds of times until my knees resemble bombed craters.

About bathrooms. They are not filthy because they don't have any in Paris. If they had any they'd probably be filthy. But every corner has a pissoir for MEN, small round structures. Men simply walk in and pee. On the bottom, I see their shoes and hear their manly noises. Mutti and I must return to our hotel each time.

"Women need to pee also," I complain to Vati who is a man and should know. He commiserates, but that's all, and it is not enough.

The next day, the unthinkable happens. I can't hold it, pull up my skirt and pee between two cars, my butt towards passing cars, my front facing stranger's faces, right on the Champs-Élysées in the middle of Paris! Mad as hell, I find a new hobby: pissing off those pissing in the pissoirs by untying their shoelaces, especially those of fancy shoes. Those annoy me the most. Then I run like hell to the next one. Mutti does not try this being a lady, but she doesn't heartily discourage me either with her faint Mona Lisa smile.

· · ·

One very hot day we visit Versailles. All these rooms with gold and jewels, even Vati shakes his head.

"This is the epitome of decadence."

"What does that mean?"

"It's when luxuries become necessities." He enjoys making me think. I wouldn't mind a bit of my own decadence, not too much like the princess did, wouldn't want my head to roll in the dirt or anywhere.

There is a golden throne for the king's private business. Mutti explains "The drawer below the seat caught what he thought smelled superior to anybody else's. The epitome of arrogance."

"Did someone have to wipe him?"

"The royal butt wiper," jokes Vati. "The perfect job for you." I sneer at him.

Mutti points at the boots and the wigs.

"In summer, the palace must have stunk like a latrine, and those petticoats held by a cage of steel! Imagine walking under such weight and breathing inside their tight corsets!"

Vati is amused. "How clever. Women couldn't run away, and they couldn't talk too much."

I could listen all day to life before me. But it is time to pack up and go to the beach with Ulla and the parents and see Gernot. I've missed my big brother

20

THE OCEAN AND A HEART AFLUTTER

An overwhelming quiet awakens me. Where is the scenery of sounds I got accustomed to? The rattling and snorting of garbage trucks and motorbikes, the ears piercing whistles of police? Instead, there's a faint rhythmic sound, the taking in of air and crashing it back out. It must be the ocean. We arrived late last night in this quaint little cottage. A quick breakfast of a baguette dipped into milky coffee, and we're on our way.

"Right around the corner you'll get your first glimpse," says Vati, shaking his finger to underline the importance of his words. I can't imagine so much water with no land behind to hold it in, and I stop to catch every detail of this moment before slowly peeking around the white walls of the corner building to a vision beyond any dreams. The ocean, dancing a mesmerizing waltz with the sun, exploding, sparkling and stunningly alive in its fury to get ashore. Above, a blue sky stretches and blends into the horizon in a seamless line. Gently swaying palms and white sands frame this moment for me forever. It is a life altering moment. How can so many different worlds be in this one world? War and peace side by side, misery and joy, and even giraffes. How I love giraffes.

The air is salty and filled with the vibes of happy people. They elegantly air kiss each other's cheeks. Germans squeeze your hand till it hurts. And I know, right at that corner: one day, I shall live in such a world.

Mutti is waiting at the next corner. She watched me dream.

"Mutti," is all I can say.

"It's amazing, isn't it?" And she takes my hand as we silently enter my new world.

We swim, we eat, build sandcastles and swim again. Gernot, who has joined us, finds a girl, Janine, with the tiniest bikini and boobs that look like those things Mutti bakes with yeast. And, like in a fairy tale, this beautiful story includes a girl who meets a handsome boy, and their first love is sprouting like a weed, fast and forgettable. His name is Michel, a dark haired, browned to a tasty crisp twelve-year old with eyes like magnets. He wears a tiny bathing trunk, wraps me into his arms and slings a black cape around us, his intoxicating aura ripe with a pungent scent. We have no words for he speaks French, but who needs words. We strut along the beach, two young fledglings feeling an early quickening in our veins.

When his family leaves there are no broken hearts. There will be more first loves, I feel it in my gut and see it on the beach: so

many dark- haired boys with the skin of buttered pretzels!
Maybe next time I can even talk to the guy!

It's a great summer for Gernot, Ulla and me. But Mutti and
Vati are often distracted and sad, like when they don't seem to
hear me, or they stare into the distance and don't see me either.
That's when they think of Hartmut, and I wait a few moments
till they come back and see me.

21

FIRST IMPRESSION FALL 1953

Millions of years before the advent of balls of any kind, a ball busting fiery volcano loomed over what is now known as Bad Godesberg, a picturesque town with an old ruin perched on top of a small hill, a faint reminder of the great volcano. There are springs and baths with sulfurous, healing waters. There is the mighty river Rhein with its beautiful backdrop of the Seven Mountains, and then there is my family, only five of us now.

We just moved to our new German capital and into our own brand-new home. We are lucky. The government itself is still in dire need of shelter as are the thousands of people moving here to find jobs and homes. All my life we were stuffed like Sauerkraut into tight refugee quarters, and I am in awe at what we have now! A two-story home with a real bathroom and a separate toilet, a large yard and the most beautiful tiled fireplace in the hallway the color of the late setting sun.

. . .

During all those weeks at the beach I never missed Hartmut. He lived in the powerful waves that crashed against the sand, in the vastness of the ocean, and all thought of him turned into something larger than death. It's different here at home. It's his pillowcase with its familiar spot of dried saliva and old age, his favorite blanket, and his death keeps clinging like a scent we can't wash off. Sometimes I tell him about the boys at the beach, their tiny bathing trunks where I didn't quite know where to look. Their skin so dark and glistening in the sun, sending out such intoxicating aromas. How I wanted to take a bite out of them!

He always listens to me.

Most of our neighborhood is under construction. But two corners down and next to the river Rhein is an area of large new buildings for Americans and foreign diplomats. It dwarfs our own. They are built into a parklike setting without any fences. A most welcoming sight, I think. Could our thoughts, too, be fenced in instead of being free to roam and explore? Here the roads are roomy enough for the most amazingly dreamy cars in soft pink, turquoise, blue and purple, some with wings opened to the sun like petals of a flower. Street cruisers we call those. If I had a gigantic yard, I'd landscape it with these colorful cars. They'd bloom year-round and wouldn't ever need weeding or watering.

The steady roar of the river is powerful and distinct, written by a different composer than the one who created the rhythm of the oceans. I can see spending much time along its shore riding my bike, dreaming and thinking, even in drizzly weather like today when earthworms crawl around with their musty odor of decay. If you break one in half, both halves crawl away. It makes me strangely melancholy and thoughtful. Why would I want to break a worm in half? Maybe he likes his life.

Now that Hartmut is dead, Gernot bugs me to play chess with him.

"You are almost ten, you could learn it, you know, you are relatively smart," he says.

I don't like the sound of it and try it on him.

"You are relatively handsome. And stop asking, stupid donkey!" He is close to sixteen, very handsome with a low, melodious voice and hands and feet as big as bear paws. Ulla bosses me around, nags me to put my stuff away, although we have hardly any stuff.

"Stuff it yourself," I yell, "I wish we had more stuff, I'd stuff it up your butt."

And Mutti doesn't say a word. We are all not ourselves.

Since we went to France, Ulla has turned away from me in the morning. I know she has grown a big dark bush in front and tries to hide it. Mutti, who sleeps in the living room with Vati, she turns around too. I think she feels less naked with her butt pointed at us. She is right. Her front looks spooky. Her breasts need fluffing up and her patch of hair is like straw! Vati doesn't seem to mind. He helps her in the morning tightening her corset made with real whale bones and his hands like to linger on her skin.

Oma is visiting for a few days to 'cheer us up.' First, she sews curtains. They turn our house into a nest. I like it! Next, she sews a couple of colorful dresses for Mutti who still wears her dark skirt and jacket.

"Put them on," she says. "The color will cheer you up. Then we can all feel better."

Mutti, slightly rattled, does what she is told. And when she sees our faces light up with joy, she keeps them on.

"Very nice," murmurs Vati into her neck when he comes home, and she hides away her dark things. I tell Hartmut about it. He seems relieved. He just wants to be a memory now.

22

INDOCTRINATION AND INDECENCY

J utta is the most freckled girl I ever met, with a smile like a slice of apple. She is my first but short-lived friend who shares her books with me. We are all hungry for books and share whatever is left after the war. I start to devour the first one with its stories and pictures of beautiful blonde women and children knitting socks and mittens for the war effort. Their men, gorgeous blonde heroes in uniform, come home for short visits to get them pregnant. When one dies, they make their family proud. I can't stop reading. Vati peeks over my shoulder.

"What bullshit. Life is too short to waste on such crap."

"I really love the crap."

Mutti takes one look at the book, enough to know what it's about. The blondes, the soldiers, flags and Jesus on the cross.

"Of course you do, Sunshine, it's called indoctrination."

"You are trying to indoctrinate ME!"

"Indoctrination narrows your mind. Learning is to expand it," says Vati, shaking his index finger at me.

Mutti says to go read it and decide for myself.

After the first two books, I realize how it teaches you to love war, soldiers and God like they belong together, and I don't want to read the next fourteen volumes. Jutta hands me another book instead, 'Heidi and the Powder Puff.'

Mutti shakes her head. "Soon we'll get you good books, Sunshine, I promise."

It's a sunny day. I go outside to join my three new friend boys in a game of soccer. They suggest we go play in the thicket behind our houses instead. Maybe because I kick hard but mostly in the wrong direction. We run to the little thicket, an old overgrown apple orchard, and play tag and hide and seek, and I climb a tree all the way to the top. When I look down, three boys are staring up my skirt, a bit retarded looking, tongues sticking out like overheated dogs and I quickly slide back to the ground.

"Want to play doctor?" asks the husky and whitest one. How, I wonder?

"You show us your girl parts, and we show you our thing."

They don't even know what to call it!! A thing, that poor little thing!

"Don't you know its name? I've seen it many times."

I feel sorry for them. We are sitting in the dirt together, my skinny legs sticking out from under my skirt, the pleated one. Should I lift it? Let them have a glimpse? Nobody moves. I am a patient person but only for very short moments, and I grab my skirt ready to show my thing – do I even have a thing? – and realize that I've never seen my own privates. I should look at them before showing them to strangers. And what's up with their thing?

I get up, strut away, full of myself and my good sense. After all, high school will start soon. And, I wonder, what are those things really called? Mutti calls them dingdong and a flower. Darn it. Those names are for kids. I don't know either. They must be way special.

At home, I point between my legs.

"Mutti, I itch. What is that thing called?"

"You itch, go wash."

"But what is it called?"

"Your Blümchen."

No. It is not a little flower! Highly annoyed, I stomp upstairs to wash. I don't even itch. And like pesky mosquitoes, those elusive boy and girl words will hover around me in their void till the day I'll learn their names.

Gradually, I am blending into the neighborhood. If I wore grey clothes to match the sky, I might become invisible.

23

AUTUMN 1953

Summer is moving over for fall. The first leaves are changing their color much as my life will change today. Mutti walks me to my new school, a Gymnasium, where I'll spend the next nine years of my life. She wears her colorful new dress and sensible shoes. I don't like sensible shoes. They are ugly and last forever. But I am excited about school, wishing only for clean bathrooms and that the safety pin in my skirt won't pop. If it does, my skirt will drop and bare my buttocks. 'Your butt talks,' laughs Ulla when I fart.

Back at home, during the midday meal of potatoes, carrots and liver, I brag about school, its theatre and science labs, the teachers and the toilets.

"They are clean enough to lick." I look at Mutti. Ours don't sparkle. Ours are barely clean!

"You may lick my butt if you want. It tastes of bacon," volunteers Ulla.

Gernot thinks "More like big as a bus with diesel fumes."

"Kids, we are at the table." Mutti tries to sound stern but fails. Hers is an easy laugh but ever so close to her easy melancholy.

Today is November the 21st, my tenth birthday. Vati wakes me up, the first to congratulate me. He rubs his unshaven chin against my neck and chest till I squeal for mercy. I am now a two-digit person and will remember this day forever, the day I started to act more grown up, be dignified, fart with less fanfare. With such high goals in my mind, I jump out of bed, get ready and go downstairs. There is a present, wrapped in wrinkled tissue paper and tied with an old red shoelace. My first real present! I eat my cereal and run to school, wondering what it might be. What would I even want? I can't think of a single thing, but my hopes are as high as the liquored- up lady at the corner window whose sad ramblings are even louder than usual.

In the evening, Mutti takes off her apron and, with the smell of cake up my nose, we sing 'Happy Birthday.' Very slowly, to squeeze out every drop of joy, I unwrap my present. It is long, very long. It looks poisonous. It's a snake with nasty squares in hues of brown and orange. Hideous. These are stockings. Nobody wears those.

"They are made of pure wool. They'll keep you toasty warm in winter. Do try them on, ja?" Mutti looks at me so very hopeful. I slowly pull them over my ankles, my knees and above, hook them into my garter belt, hating every inch of them. I hate them so much I can't even tell if they are ugly or not. Mutti and Ulla love them and Vati loves what they love. Gernot nods approvingly. He knows a lot about things like stockings and legs.

"They are pretty. It's your legs that look funny."

I stick out my tongue. They ruined my birthday and all my good intentions! Ach! I so loved my present when it was wrapped. After dinner, in the silence of the night, I go outside, kneel onto the gravely ground and rub until the stockings are in shreds. Back inside, I say

"Mutti, the stockings broke."

"They what?" One look at my knees and Vati slams his fist on the table, jumps out of his seat in a scary shade of anger and digs his fingers into my arm.

"How could you!"

"I couldn't help myself, I am sorry," and maybe I am a little sorry, since his fingers are shredding my flesh.

"There won't be any other stockings this winter," says Mutti, teary eyed.

Vati sends me upstairs to bed. Then they play my birthday games and eat MY cake. They are laughing and happy without me which is worse even than the stockings. Were those truly as ugly as I thought? I have no clue. I am a thoughtless stubborn goose with no taste of my own. How could I! I cry myself to sleep, knowing that I did wrong.

A sunny morning awakens me to the chirping of birds, the smell of coffee, and to my own deep shame. I can only hope last night was my last childish episode. Tail between my legs, too proud to apologize but reasonably polite, I mingle downstairs.

And when they are all very friendly to me, staying grumpy is getting so hard it's annoying me all over again.

A few days later, to my horror, several people parade around school in those exact stockings. They become popular and those orange and brown squares look so very pretty. It hurts me to the core. I tell myself what a good lesson it was, but to tell the truth, I don't get me.

'And they are so warm,' I'm told, as I wear my darned, washed out grey stockings that fit only for being so old and stretched.

But, as planned, my birthday was a day to remember!

24

THE OLD MAN AND HIS CAR

"Let's serenade him while doing the dishes."

I wish I could be like Ulla, kind and thoughtful. She opens our kitchen window where our neighbor, a shy and spindly man, is washing his tiny car. A chunk of his cheek got blown off in the war! Ulla washes and I dry our yellow plates and bowls with their spidery cracks while singing to him. Ulla is great at harmonizing. I am good at singing very loud and he keeps washing his clean car.

We quickly learn more songs and opera arias. Ulla is into it with passion, her shiny eyes bouncing off my high notes. Soon we give him real concerts, every day after the midday meal. And he is always there, rain or shine, washing his tiny car which he barely uses. Maybe he comes out to hear us? I put the fire of Italian divas into the high notes and all three of us are happy. Really, there is nothing more fun than doing dishes with Ulla!

. . .

"Girls." Mutti is sticking her head in the door. "You do some lovely singing, and for the whole neighborhood, but remember quiet time between one and three. Maybe tone down the high notes a bit?"

Quiet time in Germany is like a religion. We believe in it. Dogs are kept in-doors, music gets turned down and the quiet turned way up. Germans get so quiet you barely know they exist. But only during those hours!

25

BOYS, BREASTS AND BODY
PARTS 1954

Boys! I do love them, love when they look at me, when our eyes meet in a knowing kind of way. I wish I understood what it's about. There is this boy who keeps staring at me during English class with a face to feast on. Dark skin with golden curls a bit on the wild side. I like that he likes me and take quick peeks to make sure he is still looking. In my dreams, he smells like the oil Vati rubs on his hair.

One day, I check to see if he is looking. He stares right at me while digging in his nose. Not just a quick pick like I do, but he digs and pokes, he jabs and pulls, and it's a slug, and he eats it as if it were a Schneckenudel. Ach. He picked the romance right out of his nose and ate it. And that's the end of him.

Early one morning, my family decides to go to the Seven Mountains for a long hike. It will be a hot and muggy day and we aim for a deep cold quarry lake surrounded by high cliffs to swim off the sweat and eat our 'Butterbrot.'

A beautiful ferry ride across the Rhein takes us to the Seven Mountains. My eyes are drawn to the long river barges, often several of them tied together as if holding hands. Families live aboard year-round, clotheslines strung across, laundry flapping in the wind, and we hear faint voices and the laughter of kids as they are gliding by on the water of the Rhine in its impatient rush to the sea.

On the other side, our narrow path is winding past willow trees and old homes from a time when people were shorter, and on into a forest of firs. We walk single file and I, at eleven, topless. Three young men hike towards us and six beady boy eyes latch like magnets onto my breasts. In a flash, my hands fly up to cover what were two flat pancakes seconds ago. Suddenly I have breasts, stared into existence by their eyes and I am naked with a shirt made of goose bumps and a new body odor worse than Gernot's. At home, a heavy sweater helps regain my dignity and for now, I banish my breasts forever. Handsome boys confuse and startle me now more than ever, and why do they pop up everywhere like weeds?

Next day, Mutti says "Let's buy you a bra." Darn! She was walking behind me and saw their eyes on my breast. Grudgingly, I take her hand and we walk to town to buy a bra.

There is a girl at school, Hannelore, a head taller and a year older than I am. She has a loose tongue, that girl, with her lithe body and thick blonde braids. She knows things, why else would she always be whispering? The next time I see her alone, I beg her to please tell me about boys.

"It's mostly 'straightforward' that thing between their legs. It's called a penis or a 'stiffy' if it pops up." And she tells me what men do if they have a 'stiffy.' We girls have our own thing, a 'vagina,' she says, then whispers 'or pussy.' That must be the bad word the way she smirks! I still have never seen mine and nothing pops up.

Penis and vagina, such pretty names. I could see naming a boy and girl with those names IF they didn't mean penis and vagina, but they do, and I think 'pokey penis properly pickled' could be a tongue twister.

"More like food," says Hannelore. "Pickled, huh."

The new words are powerful. At night, they rock me into a sleep of seductive imagery of sounds and shapes and open a door to strong new feelings. There's a soft awakening in my private parts, a tiny pulse. I put my hand to it, my own little nest, safe and warm.

Next morning, so many more questions are 'popping up.'

But Hannelore has taught me all she knows.

26

THE HORRORS OF HISTORY 1955

In fairy tales, bad guys get their head chopped off. In real-life, they become politicians. I think fairy tales handle it way better.

Another 100,000 prisoners are released from a Russian prison camp. Mutti buys more food and extra butter and cheese. She seems strangely agitated as if the war were coming closer again. Daily, one or two men ring the doorbell. It's hard to watch them lean on crutches and manage food, harder to see the cold fear of war still crippling them more than their blown off limbs. Fear has an odor, you know. Animals smell it and I think so do I. It surrounds them, invisible, untouchable, and hides in their sunken eyes that tell of things only they can see. They come with their stinking bodies, day after day. I don't believe in God, but I do think about him a lot these days. Would like him to know that war is a load of crap. They are starving. Really. How can we help when they need so much more than we can give? So much more than food. And day after day they come and beg.

. . .

"Always offer them food but give them no money. They'd likely buy liquor with it. Couldn't really blame them," says Mutti.

I quickly run to the door when the bell rings. It might be one of them. I fix bread with butter and cheese, sometimes just bread with butter since that's all there is, and we will be needing some too. I do this wretched job for the sense it gives me of war's sorrow and lunacy, and their faces are engraved in my soul. Their numbers slowly dwindle, then stop.

Only one man ever was angry for not getting money. He limped away swearing God awful stuff.

Only one man said, "I have a daughter, might be your age."

And his look of longing stung me deep inside.

I have a dream. Full of questions about life, I am in a circus sitting on a sky swing with long chains. It rises higher and higher, around and around into the balmy air currents above, where all my questions find answers. I am filled with bliss and satisfaction. When I wake up floating inside this heavenly current, the questions and their answers have vanished into the ether.

Mutti and Vati are sending Ulla and me to the movies. Movies are like stuffed cabbage, a rare treat, and I fall in love with most leading men if they aren't too old.

"No, no, these are real-life films with the actual people. Documentaries of camps, not what you think. It's bad. Horrible stuff." Vati coughs up his anger and pain loud enough to wake a dead person and puts a quick damper on Ulla's and my fantasies.

"It will break your heart," says Mutti. "But we want you to see and feel what it was about. It is too painful to describe with words." She follows us out the door, her blue eyes laced with worry. Silently, Ulla and I walk to the theatre. She looks solemn. I am disappointed, wanted to drool over a handsome face and well-tanned muscles. Instead, we enter an empty theatre. Only a handful of young adults are scattered about the large room with none of the usual chatter, and the air turns oppressive in this ominous sea of empty seats, almost as if it were part of the movie, 'the emptiness of war.'

When the movie begins our breathing slows, our stomachs twist into knots, overwhelmed by emotions and disbelief. My fingers start to claw into Ulla's arm, my feet tighten into balls and my face cradles into her shoulder. There is a whole other world within the world I know, the dark side hiding all around us, cruel and evil, multiplying like a fungus, waiting to pop out when the time is propitious. I don't know how to feel so much misery, how to be sad enough.

At the end, we want to hold still in the quiet dark, haunted and sick by what we saw, but bright lights chase us out and our swollen eyes find comfort in the cool and drizzly night air. We walk home in total stillness, close to each other. It is a dark night with only a sliver of the moon. There are no words left nor any emotions, only a raw emptiness. At home, we hug.

Next morning, I wake up to the unbearable burden of being me, a German.

. . .

Outside, the light drizzle turned into heavy rain. It furiously pelts the windows, and trees are bending from the weight of the wind. My heart aches from last night's movie. Mutti is watching me. She pats the space next to her on the old flowery sofa, and I squeeze with all my might into her body with its subtle scent of powder. Now her eyes are staring back in time and I remain silent until she turns to me.

"I was a bit of an oddball, you know. I was eighteen when I met the only true friends I ever had, Trudy, Lilly, and Vera. So long ago now. We danced together at the Stuttgart Opera house and their large families welcomed me like their own. Beautiful, generous people all of them. It was the best time of my life. I was independent, made money, fell in love with Vati. Ach!" She barely whispers. "They were Jewish."

"Did they get away?" She shakes her head, teardrops spilling down her cheek. "Their families were well known. They didn't think it would happen to them. Ach, Sabinchen." She clutches me closer and her salty tears are wet against my blouse.

This is how Mutti spends her Sunday afternoons when she rests on her yellow easy chair and Vati reminds us to leave her be. I can see it, with the same lost look. On Sundays, she is with Trudy, Lilly, and Vera, and I look at her differently now. Through her ageing face and greying hair, I see and feel how she was young, full of ideas and passions, a bit flirty. How she had life figured out until it took off like a raging river, and all she could do was hold on and stay afloat. And it hurts me and stings, because of her pain and the horror and all our shame.

. . .

I am now a faithful reader of the daily news, mesmerized by politics. Vati and Mutti start to explain things to me now. I feel in my heart that all those bits and pieces of news yanked from random conversations when lines were long and food was scarce, and caught from whispers not meant for me, that finally those lifelong questions will be answered. About time! The knot in my heart, grown of those whispers and innuendoes since birth, was ready to explode.

FLIES IN THE FOOD AND OTHER DELICACIES

I am twelve years old and my parents enroll me in a summer camp at the Baltic Sea. For the next four weeks, I will live amidst lovely pines above water's edge, with horses, healthy meals and sports. As soon as I arrive, I ask to see the horses.

"Sorry, we got rid of them. They were too dangerous," says a young woman who looks like a horse. Having never been spoiled, I am not mad. There is still the Baltic Sea. It won't be so easy to get rid of, even if it proves to be wet and menacing.

How wrong I am!

Down the hill and through the pines is the Sea. Except, we may only go to our knees. My wrath is rising like well shaken beer and I slowly wade into the water over slippery rocks. It is freezing, melted snow from Sweden feeding into it. But I go on till I am far enough to swim. And I swim till an ugly voice in an ugly face comes after me in a rowboat. "You can't do that!"

"We paid for horses and swimming," I yell back.

.　.　.

What else can possibly happen? Dinner time happens, with a vegetable soup drenched in flies. Tiny flies with wings and legs, dead and by the hundreds. I pick them out, then I eat. Most others don't eat at all. In the morning, we get leftover vegetable soup for breakfast. With hardly anybody eating, the soup will last all week.

"Let's run away," I say to my bunkmate Helga. "We can go to Denmark, it's not far, and maybe to Norway." She is all in, and a third girl wants to pay for everything if we take her too. We decide to leave at naptime.

You can see us now, walking to town on a sandy path amongst pines. Helga and I with the swagger of explorers, Karin limping along, fearful.

"Those flies must really BUG you," I tease her but get no smile.

In town, she pays for our tickets and we embark the small ferry to Denmark, get off after a calm ride under sunny skies, and walk to the border. We try to charm our way through but fail miserably. Two men in black suits, lying in wait, take us back in a shiny black car. Silently, they drive us to a 2-story house in the town of Eckernförde, near the main sandy beach. It stands full of old charm amidst summer flowers and under a canopy of trees. It's where the pastor lives.

"Talk," he says curtly, after taking us into his study.

"You can't take us back to the camp," I say. "Those people lied. There are no horses, we can't swim, and flies swim in the soup. Hundreds of little flies with wings and legs. Flies should be flying. It's not moral," I say, hoping it's clear that I am pissed but with dignity.

"Ach," he says, waving his hand like trying to swat one, then turns to the window that his pretty yard may yield him answers.

Meanwhile, the government in Bonn has been notified of three runaway girls from a summer camp at the Baltic Sea. It's big news in the offices of our small government.

"One of them is my daughter, I know it," says Vati as soon as he hears about it. "There must have been a problem for her to do that. They'll be alright. It's not her first time."

He can't wait to get home and tell Mutti, who laughs.

"Of course, it's Sabine. They'll have a great adventure."

The pastor looks happy when he turns around. He invites us to stay at his home, take all our meals at the house, enjoy the beach and the town. He trusts us 'to stay together at all times and be inside before dark.'

We are shown to a gabled room upstairs, with curtains and blankets made of the same flowery print. It looks awfully pretty. And we get the best food ever, fit for a king, a pastor and for us. No wonder his stomach is well curved like a harvest moon. Never in my life was there so much food anywhere close to me. Meats, desserts, fruits, nut bread.

Karin wonders whether I was scared talking to the pastor. I tell her I enjoyed it.

"You are weird," she says.

"You want to be normal? Go back and eat flies," I tell her off.

We while away the rest of our time swimming, boy watching, walking through the pretty town eating ice cream thanks to Karin's money, and writing postcards. Then we swim and boy watch again.

Back at home, Vati, who would have loved to be an explorer, says "Too bad they didn't let you see Denmark."

Mutti hugs me with a big smile, her blue eyes full of sparkle.

"Go wash your hands, Sunshine, I made your favorite meal, liver, carrots with peas and mashed potatoes."

Both are proud of me for fighting for my right to a good vacation.

28

THE IMPORTANCE OF COLORS

D id I hear right? '.... Babies.....stolen....' I rush into the room to my parent's muffled voices.

"Whose babies? What happened?" I plop down hard into Mutti's soft body. Her eyes are filled with profound sadness as she puts her hand on mine. Vati's pointy elbows rest on his knees.

"Ach," he explains. "Nazis tried to breed blonde and blue-eyed babies. They called it 'Lebensborn,' or 'fount of life.'

I know how our body parts with their pretty names fit together, but Hannelore left out the thing about choosing colors.

"How do you have to do it to get the color right?" I wonder.

"Blonde parents are likely to produce blonde babies." Mutti gets up and rushes out the door, agitated. Her grim face leaves a gloom in the room, and her hefty bottom a dent on the cushion.

Vati clears his throat. It doesn't need cleaning, it's emotional muck is what it is.

"If one had to breed, it should be the brightest not the whitest." And that's all I learn.

. . .

The thought of those blonde babies lingers on in the days to come.

At night, however, boys sneak into my dreams. Dark boys like the ones on the beach in France. The few white ones looked naked is how I saw them, like plucked chickens. Cluck cluck.

On Sunday, our only day off from school, we go hike in the Kottenforst, our forest above town, even under drizzly skies like today. Mutti points to the subtle beauty of autumn colors. I prefer the frivolous amount of color and scent of spring and summer flowers, meant for the mating season, I bet. It is why humans, mostly Americans, paint their lips and add perfume. Life is about making babies! One large party the world over humping away, each of us a piece of a puzzle trying to fit and feast together, even on each other, in harmony. People, animals, fish and rats.

It is windy and the tall trees seem to be humming. Then the whole forest is chiming in and I swing my hips and hum along. Music makes me do it. Mutti smiles. Maybe she hears it too? I love when she is happy, and I use the moment to ask about the stolen babies and why the church didn't help.

"The Pope was on Hitler's side, you know. Bad things happened, Sunshine, bad things."

She picks up the pace trying to run away from me and those bad things. Why? What about it makes her so uneasy?

. . .

A few days later, Vati and I walk to town. There's a man in front of us. His hands stick out of his army uniform. They are of a deep black. And his head is covered in short and tight black curls. How would they feel to touch? Soft, or bristly like Vati's morning chin? His neck is black too. I guess he is black all around. I imagine him naked but just for a moment. It seems private!

"What would happen if I married a black man?"

"I'd rather you marry a smart and kind black than a dumb white."

Of course. Why did I even ask?

29

TWO ANGRY MEN AND ONE
CRAZY VATI

Hefty knocks and excessive ringing of the bell make me run to the door. Two men, young tall hunks, rudely ask for Herr Birkholz while stepping right through me into the house. Vati pokes his head out of the living room. They don't ask but tell him to go inside for privacy and all three disappear behind the door. Something is said, I can't hear, but Vati's angry scream cuts through the air like a sword as he opens the door.

"Get out!"

A couple of weeks later the same nasty bullies are back, push their way into the house and to the living room. Look at them, blonde with fat necks and dull eyes, heavy from beer and sausages. Two hoodlums stuffed into elegant new suits and fedora hats, like sprinkling sugar on a pile of shit. Vati is ready. He meets them at the living room door, livid, his strong hand dragging the first one by the arm through the hallway and throwing him down the two steps of the entry. Back in, he grabs the next one who was about to leave on his own, and throws him out too, yelling from the top of his voice

"Tell your Nazi boss to come himself. I'll throw him out, too."

Nobody ever comes back.

"What did they want? Why are they coming after you now?"

"German bureaucracy. They found my name in some records and want to investigate me for anti-German activities. Anti Hitler, that is, in 1955! Surreal. I went to two communist party meetings before the war but never went back. Their propaganda was as hateful as the Nazis'."

"So, what now?"

"You tell me! They could investigate me for not following orders to go east to keep the Russians out! We would all be dead, together with 170,000 others that did go. We escaped that night. Don't worry. These Nazi generals are trying to intimidate me. I treat them politely enough but don't go drinking, don't respect them and do not salute any of these... ach. Swines."

I have never seen Vati scared. When faced with a scary dog like a Rottweiler drooling over which part of his leg to bite into, he goes down on all fours and growls back till the dog retreats. Most likely, dogs are not scared of him as a dog but rather of him as a crazy person. That's what scares them!

The next morning, Vati's dark curls are speckled with grey as he reads the news! When did that happen? And his bald spot is growing like the waxing moon. It smells of a lotion he keeps rubbing on. Apparently, it works wonders, and soon all his hair will be rubbed off. Who is he? I know hardly anything about him!

In the evening I squeeze onto the sofa between him and Mutti. She is mending a sock over a wooden egg. I sniff Vati's hair.

"I love your baldness," I say. "Tell me about your first memory when you were little."

He puts down his book, thinks for a moment, then he begins.

"When I was six years old, WWI was raging. Times were hard. The Red Cross took me and a hundred hungry little boys on a long train ride to a large farm in Romania. They put us into pig sties in the middle of hundreds of little pigs. It was the happiest time of my life, all six weeks of Summer. We lived with them, played and rolled around dirty, smelly, all the way from head to toe and happy to the core. The farmers treated us well and gave us good food. But we lived with those pigs, and I have never been sick since."

"Those that survived will likely have eternal life," says Mutti.

"More, tell me more." He stares at me with his intense green eyes, like he saw me for the first time, or maybe he sees me as an almost adult.

"Well then. When I was sixteen, we lived in a small village in the South. On Saturdays we bathed, and on Sundays we went to church like everybody. One Sunday, I said

"Mother, I don't want to go." She wondered why.

"I don't feel like it." She seemed baffled and said I must go in case it's true.

"In case it's true? Mother, might it not be true?"

"Well, I think it is, but I don't know. It's only a belief. You must believe."

"But why?"

And again, she said "just in case."

This talk changed my life. The absurdity of 'just in case' hit me hard. It freed my mind from the talons of the church to question all thoughts. Before graduation, counselors suggested I'd make a great preacher and it was a good living.

"I stopped believing," I said. They replied, 'belief is not required!' Imagine that!"

"But you are our very own preacher," I tell him. Vati laughs out loud.

Mutti warns me. "He tries to be. Don't be his or anybody's sheep, ever!"

Vati continues. "Next I studied languages, history and philosophy in Munich, Paris and Heidelberg. I heard Hitler speak. His ideas of supremacy and his war mongering were as clear as they were bone chilling. He yelled how he'd make Germany great again. People cheered, ignored the devil in the details. Dumb folks."

"Why didn't you leave Germany?"

"I did. Before I met your Mother. Nazism had spread like a virus, and one day, with only the clothes on my back, I biked south to get away."

"I would so love to do that. Really, I want to...."

"Don't ever do that. Do you hear me?"

"Yes, you scream right in my ear."

"Sorry. I biked all the way through France, worked at farms for shelter and food, and ended up in a small fishing village in Spain. Spent a memorable year amongst the kindest people. But politics under General Franco, a madman bad as Hitler, made me bike back to Germany where I met your Mother. Then you all showed up and I stayed. Lucky you!"

HOT BROTHERS AND HOT PANTIES

The Gruber brothers arrived at my school, and life will never be the same again. Robert, he is the husky one with blonde fuzz over very pouty lips and a touch of bow legged. I bet he plays soccer and then his skin will taste salty. He towers over his younger brother Werner, who is elegant and darkish, a secret spy in my dreams. He is two years older than I am. Both are naughty looking, so very naughty looking. Just thinking about them, and my heart stops and races and sputters along.

School is my other world, my very own Taj Mahal of love. I love everybody and feel loved by everybody, feel a healthy sense of my own self, strong and secure, with the knowledge that I count, and an amazing feeling of approaching adulthood. Until I see those handsome devils, the Gruber brothers. Lately, when I feel their eyes on me, I morph into pure sweet jello, my spine a useless, spineless thing. During class when my dreams take me on trips around their bodies, and in such private ways, it gets downright scandalous. And I so like it. Could other kids have similar feelings and dreams? Nobody ever talks about such things.

"Sabine, are you dreaming again?" asks Herr Stahl.

"Sorry."

He shakes his bald head, the color of a peeled potato. He sees no hope in teaching algebraic formulas to thirty squirmy adolescents. None whatsoever!

On the way home, both brothers are standing on the corner staring at me and up and down and I don't know how to walk, where to look. Every part of my body comes alive with a fire, including, you know, down there with the pretty name. Robert, the older, rugged one, asks if I want to go to a party. I shake my head and follow my feet straight home. Darn it, why did they ask? I wish they would have just carried me off!

At home, I blush at random and barely talk. One look at me and Gernot grins his boyish grin.

"You are love struck, little sister. Watch out for bad boys. All boys are bad boys."

Mutti studies me. She is thinking and cooking up an idea! Darn! After washing the last yellow plate with its spidery cracks, barely serenading the neighbor, I head upstairs to our bedroom, climb on top of our bunk bed, dangle down my legs, and think about the two brothers. What if they are bad? What is so bad about bad? Mutti says Vati was a bad boy. Then she smiles.

They are laughing downstairs. Probably about my hormones and goo goo eyes for boys.

The smell of chicken soup squeezes through the heater vent and mixes with the sound of Ulla's newest pastime, playing the violin. Who would have thought? Chicken and violin, a powerful and intriguingly confusing combination of smell and sound and I think about how hard it is to be a girl.

It's hard to be a girl, not a child, not a woman, just a girl. Torn between the two, belonging to neither.

It's hard to be a girl, a stranger in my own body. Proud and gutsy one moment, fragile the next like the fluffy down of a feather.

It's tough to be a girl, when you want to howl at night like a love-struck cat making babies in the moonshine.

It's hell to be a girl when your love comes out as piss and vinegar, and you don't know how to turn it into wine.

But I love to be a girl, treasure the pieces of me handed down by generations, and I'll squeeze in the new pieces that are my very own until they fit.

I feel a big awakening, like my family, who are they? Do they like me and why? When I admire the night sky, nestled in Vati's arms and see its infinite possibilities, I feel a thrill of things, an awe that might be religion. My own one. I am alive inside this bubble that's our universe and greater than all there is. I wonder what lies behind that bubble. There must be more. Even if there is an end, there must be a new beginning, another bubble and another, like soap bubbles. With so many thoughts in my pea sized brain, compared to the universe, I am challenging teachers and family alike, arguing all day long about anything. My teachers don't seem to mind, neither does Vati.

"We argue because we are full of questions and opinions," he says, "but to argue means to listen half the time and you, Sabine, give me the shorter half."

Other times he calls me Xanthippe. I finally check the lexicon. She was the cantankerous wife of Socrates. Really!

In the evening, Mutti starts to knit a strange pink thing. What is it? What in heaven or hell is she knitting? Her needles go 'clickclickclick.'

"Mutti, what are you.... please, and in pink?"

"It's going to be really warm underwear for you girls in winter. Real thick wool, and it will go way past your garter belt hooks so your thighs won't get cold."

"My thighs are hot."

"Of course, it's summer." She looks way too amused. She knows what I am worried about. I am not sure I know. It just seems wrong. 'Clickclick' go the needles as the yarn glides through her fingers and the first leg grows to enormous proportions. My butt will look like a big pink poodle. The hot day turns into a chilly nightmare! Mutti is worried about my virtue!

Vati has his own thoughts about keeping me busy. He agreed to make a new German/French dictionary.

"Sabine, you could help me. You do know the alphabet, don't you?"

I won't fall for his tricks! "No, I don't."

"Then it's time you learned." And with that, I am hired. I'll be his alphabetizer. Like an appetizer made of words. Grudgingly I begin with the first box of cards.

More and more, to my surprise, I read the words. On many afternoons, for years to come, you can see me spread out on the living room floor amongst hundreds of index cards, the late afternoon sun visiting my little corner, dust bunnies collecting in the pleats of my checkered skirt. Many of the words jolt my brain into new insights and thoughts beyond their definitions. Words like awesome and awful. Why is some awe good, but lots of it is, like, awful?

Meanwhile, Hannelore shares her newest boy wisdom with me.

"They do it in the 'Red Light District.' They pay a woman and then they do it."

"Can you choose which guy you want?" I think of the Gruber brothers. I want them both. But Hannelore doesn't know and all I can do is keep dreaming.

31

A BLOODY MESS 1956

I am at home when it happens, and glad about it. Drops of blood splatter into the toilet. Nasty cramps shoot through my lower parts. If this is how it's going to be, I don't want it.

"I am dying!" Mutti runs up the stairs. One look at me and she says:

"Sunshine, you're a lovely young woman now. You'll bleed every month so that you can have babies when you get married. I'll be right back with supplies."

What a feeble explanation! I can get pregnant any time I want to. I know how.

She quickly returns with napkins, shows me the way to hook them into a bloody belt and other stupid stuff, tells me to take it easy and wash every day. Then she leaves me writhing with cramps which will happen every bloody month just to have babies that I don't want. 'A lovely young woman!' Screw it!

My whole life is changing. Bloody changing!

. . .

And Oma is visiting. Not again! She looks over my shoulder like a shadow when I am in the kitchen, daring me to put my fingers in the food or lick stuff. But outside the kitchen she is good to talk to and I complain to her about belts and napkins.

"You have napkins and rubber pants? We had to make our own napkins. Layers upon layers of cotton, and still they leaked. We had to wash them by hand, boil them and string them up between houses right over our street. Like dead rats is what they looked like, chewed off and bloody dead rats. Ach. They never got clean and the guys would look up to guess who had her period. It was shameful!

Next I go to Gernot's room since he might want to be a doctor. He folds his bear sized hands and says I can get pregnant now. I beg him to tell how NOT to get pregnant.

"Put a pillow between your knees and don't let go of it." And that's what he said, I swear, and I don't know why that would work.

Ulla is even more useless. "Stay away, far away!"

She pushes with both hands against imaginary boys and men, then kicks them in the butt, her face twisted into an ugly grimace. "That's what you do, and you won't get pregnant."

To make matters of love worse, Mutti finished knitting Ulla's and my wildest underwear nightmare. Bulky, baby pink, itchy thick wool halfway down my thighs, my butt just as I feared, one big pink poodle. I am horror stricken. My life is over.

"I'll fix it," promises Ulla. The next day, after mysterious doings away from my eyes, she returns them, a large black spider stitched onto a silvery spider web right over the butt crack part and, for extra color, one green leaf. I am mad but break out laughing because it's too funny not to. Maybe in winter, who knows.... and just in case I hide them away.

32

BROAD HIPS AND NARROW MIND

"Old arrogant Nazi." Vati is allergic to his own Mother. He never visits, yet he took me to the train station to go visit his parents 'before they are too dead to meet.'

And that's where I am now, kneeling on the living room floor next to Opa, with nothing to say. He touches my head, looks at me with watery but kind eyes, his shriveled lips curved into a smile. The only hair left on his head is a soft down along his neck and fuzz in his ears, leaving the rest naked looking like wax paper. Parkinson's disease makes him tremble.

Barely an hour ago, Vati's Mother, my other Oma, picked me up at the train station in Esslingen, with a warm pretzel for a welcome. She is beautiful with a natural grace. Vati has her looks, dark with a cat's green eyes. For the midday meal, she serves crusty, juicy Ofenschlupfer (bread pudding). Then she feeds Opa his daily meal of tripe or cow stomach. I try a bit. No wonder he trembles. Like chewing old Lederhosen.

·   ·   ·

A bronze plaque on the wall, the size of a serving platter and engraved with fancy artwork, catches my eyes. Oma might be narrow minded, but her hips are broad and welcoming as she walks towards me.

"Your Opa won the bronze medal in the Olympics for ski jumping. Nine meters." Her chin is held high as if she herself had done the jumping.

For the rest of the week she serves Ofenschlupfer and pretzels for every meal. I almost forget she is a Nazi and feel bad for liking her better than my good Oma just because of the food. It seems wrong. We do not talk politics, but she tries to give me books to read, you know the ones with blondes, soldiers and God, but I don't even touch them. How can she be a Nazi with her dark hair what's left of it!

After one week, I am back home and notice things. Mutti's hair is more grey than blonde. Vati values his own opinions above all when it comes to politics, and if Mutti differs, he quickly reigns in her wayward thoughts. It's irritating. Our mind is ours. We own it.

"You should fight for your opinions," I tell her. She shrugs it off.

"I do if it matters."

Gernot grew another inch and Ulla missed me.

"He didn't listen when I sang alone," she says. "He barely washed his car."

When we do the dishes, we open the window to resume serenading our neighbor. He is waiting. And we sing our whole huge repertoire for this little man while he washes his tiny car to our rhythm. And all three of us are happy.

In the evening, I snatch Vati away from his book.

"Tell me about Opa. He had no words, only ever touched my head."

I squeeze onto the sofa in my usual spot between him and Mutti, the smell of eucalyptus oil wafting from his baldness. It's good to be back.

"Your Opa fought at the Western Front in WWI. During a short leave, he came to visit. I was six years old, and this is my very first memory of him. My younger brother Otto and I were alone. There was a knock at the door.

I see a bearded robber through the keyhole.

"Barricade," I order, dragging pillows for protection.

Otto, quiet as a mouse, pulls chairs, and then we wait in fear. Suddenly the door flings open. The bearded robber hugs our Mother, who, with familiar but trembling voice, beckons us to meet our Father."

Vati's voice is breaking and getting a bit shmaltzy from the memory but he continues.

"This bearded man remained a stranger. I could not

touch him but in secret when I was sure he would not know. Maybe he knew but felt too shy himself. After this visit, we did not see him for many years. An injury kept him in a field hospital for a whole year. He returned, shell shocked, morphed into another being. He never found meaning in his life again."

. . .

Full of emotions I cuddle close. His breath is warming my neck as he continues.

"My younger brother Otto was sent to fight in Russia. He loathed the military as did so many of his friends. He was the lucky one! He came home alive from Stalingrad on the last transport flight before the six months long battle killed two million people, including all his friends. He lives at home, shell shocked, unable to work."

Two Million, twelve Million, sixty Million. A numbing terror lives in such numbers, beyond my feelings. I am crushed by the enormity of life's sadnesses, the endless supply of horrors.

"I need fresh air," I say and get up, grab my poncho and pedal to the river. I am the only living thing riding through the silent sounds of the night, my only companion the rumbling rhythm of the low flowing river. Black slippery rocks reach like fingers far into the water, reflecting off a lone streetlight. I stop at the pretty sight. How can our enemies be enemies? We don't even know them. And I imagine the river spitting out a dark figure, a Russian enemy braving his way out of the strong currents. His long hair, the color of wet rocks, hides his pock-marked skin. He smells off rotten teeth and seaweed. I pull him out and take him home. He gulps down a piece of liver and all our potatoes, then picks up Ulla's violin and plays mournful Russian tunes.

How easily we could turn enemies into friends as long as they like liver and the violin.

The river did its magic. I feel good again.

33

A CHEESECAKE ORGY

U lla has never gotten into trouble. I would like to help her change this.

"Ulla, you should do something you can tell your kids about."

"Like what?"

I point to the cheesecake on top of the cabinet, a scrumptious piece of art meant for company later this afternoon. "We could just lick a little from the back." I move the step ladder close and go up.

"Do you think? Mutti might notice." She licks her luscious lips.

I stick my finger into the back where nobody will see unless you look, and gently pull some out and stick it in Ulla's face. She licks my finger with religious devotion and asks for just a little more. This time I use two fingers like a shovel.

"Does it show yet?" she asks.

"Only from up here. Hand me a spoon." She does and I spoon out a bunch from the middle and feed it to her.

"Still holding?" She wonders.

It takes another big spoonful for half the top to collapse. The cake looks eviscerated, abused, we feel terrible and start laughing so hard we almost pee from pleasure and panic.

"We should stuff it with a sock," suggests Ulla, "white ones to match."

Sudden footsteps. Mutti sticks in her head. One look at the stepladder, then back at us, cake smeared over our lips, chin and fingers, and she climbs up to check on her cake.

"Why for heaven's sake did you do this? You know I expect company." She is coming down the ladder, cake in hand, flustered. "I am really disappointed in you girls. What do you want me to do now?"

"Sorry, Mutti."

"Sorry, Mutti. Maybe cut away the tunneled part and serve the rest. It should be plenty," suggests Ulla. "German ladies eat too much cake."

Mutti is still shaking her head over our gluttony.

"That might work, yes," a smidgeon of a smile in her voice.

Ulla apologizes again. "Sorry, but it felt so good. It was really worth it, and I never do things like that. I can tell it to my kids."

Mutti knows she is right. She takes a knife, cuts off the damage and looks quite cheerful.

"That is good enough," she says. I bet she is already looking forward to sharing the story with the ladies.

34

THE POSTWAR YEARS

American soldiers strut around Germany. They better not be getting ready for another war! Their planes boom across the sky breaking the sound barrier with ear splitting explosions. Every time, Ulla is in a panic like the hundreds of birds that flutter and squawk and soar into the sky. I wish the Americans would go home.

But they do bring money. And money brings foreign workers, thousands of young, dark skinned men from Turkey and Italy. The way I see it, they'll work during the day, but at night, they'll take care of our millions of lonely widows and spinsters. There are not enough German men left to do the job. The irony of it! Nazis with their ideas of lily-white skin hire men that will darken us.

The new faces add color and a much-needed vibrancy to Germany. There is talk about Turkish and Italian restaurants coming to town. Signs appear on public toilets: YES' for a sitting person, a 'NO' for standing on it. Who would stand on a toilet? Then I remember the holes in France, with porcelain feet to stand in. Those foreigners might wonder why we have the hole so high up?

'It's hard to aim and one wrong move will land us in the toilet. Dumb Krauts!'

Ever so slowly, people start to talk about the past, try to find answers. How could it have happened? One has to sniff around carefully. Who is a friend? Who is not? Vati goes right to the jugular. 'When did you join the Nazi party?' he inquires, and when the person squirms uncomfortably around the question, he knows. He and Mutti have a nose for Nazis. And the Nazis, I guess, have their own nose and find their own kind. At school, talk of one's parents is taboo as is 'the Jewish question.' Except, there supposedly is a new young Jewish boy in school. I haven't seen him.

"Jews are chubby," says Heiko who has seen him.

"I didn't know you were Jewish," I say, looking him over.

"I am not. I'm Catholic, stupid."

"But you are chubby. You must be Jewish; face it, stupid." He doesn't. He is too lazy to think.

The Jewish boy does not return. I never saw him. Maybe he didn't feel safe. One day, I hope to talk about all that darn stuff with people other than my family.

There are big changes in school. I am losing the objects of my desires. The Gruber brothers, those naughty looking guys, transferred to another school and for now, my brain runs again like a well-oiled machine.

There's a new girl sitting next to me, Sieglinde, with hair so blonde it's not even a color. She is pink with short and chubby limbs. In my mind, but only in my mind, I call her a piggy. In the coming days, dark hair grows on her scalp like a layer of dirt and then, poof, it's white again. Nobody dyes their hair. Not yet, not at our age.

"What's happening to your hair?" I ask.

"Mother bleaches it." She stares straight ahead, and I leave her in peace. Not till we comfortably copy each other's home-work does she confide in me.

"Father wants me blonde. He makes Mother bleach it and I have to sleep with curlers."

"Doesn't it hurt?"

"Yes. I hate him."

When she invites me to her home, I say I hate him too because he sounds like a damn Nazi and I don't want to meet him. But it makes me wonder what happened to blonde Lebensborn babies that got dark during puberty, the way it happened to most of us? Sieglinde might be one of the babies.

35

MY FIRST JEWS 1958

"The people moving into the new house in the Moselstrasse are Jewish," shouts Gernot. He and Ulla are charged like dogs smelling a bone, ready to run and welcome them. I feel a deep apprehension. How can I look anybody Jewish in the eyes, ever? It's a bewildering thought. But I quickly follow behind. Sooner or later I got to face it.

A lady with the same elegant nose as my bad Oma opens the door. Her eyes, the color of coffee grounds, skim over us and she shakes Gernot's outstretched hand with pleasure, her dark hair brushing against her shoulders.

"You are the first to greet us. Thank you. I am Frau Strauss." She shakes Ulla's hand, then mine and, at almost fifteen, I still curtsey.

A young girl descends the stairs. I am in awe. When I come down, you can hear me. Everybody can. I slide, I jump and crash. She descends.

"Irene, my daughter, meet Gernot, Ulla and Sabine."

Gernot and Irene turn bright red. They can't even say 'hello.' Their eyes are glued to each other and his large paw swallows her tiny hand and won't let go. They just fell in love! Her eyes are like Mutti's, of the deepest blue with a glint of sapphire against her dark hair and glowing skin. I hope she has a brother!

"We will be good friends," she says with a strong French accent. She shakes Ulla's and my hand, an apparition of melody and color.

Ulla points to our house. "Please come by. On Sundays there's cake with coffee."

That's what we said, 'please come,' and Irene comes, washing up on our shores, floating into our living room and our lives. We love her, can't imagine ever not having known her. She fits into our family better than I do. She simply belongs, squeezes around the dinner table, marks her spot on our wooden corner bench, and we are tight as little birds huddling in the cold. We don't mind. Gernot and she are in love, burning to touch, and all so sudden and new. His left pinky touches her right hand with the gentleness of a butterfly to be felt by her and not seen by us.

Later in the evening, when Gernot and I brush teeth over the small sink, careful not to spit on each other's hands, I remind him to always carry a pillow.

"To squeeze between your knees, you lovesick puppy, like you told me!"

"Don't believe everything I say. If you worry, think with the brain in your head, not the one between your legs. You are responsible for your own virtue."

"And yours is under attack!" Under the influence of a strange new impulse I go hug him like adult to adult.

"Big old donkey, take care."

Ulla, meanwhile, has many suitors, the marrying kind. They come to the door with fresh haircuts. They ask for permission to take her out. Too well-mannered if you ask me, pomaded and perfumed, in full plumage like peacocks. I can't really tell who they are in real life or what to say to them. Neither does Ulla.

"Their life's vision is of a savings account and sex on Sunday. By forty we'd have our funeral planned, ready to go, with a plot and a cheap but tasteful headstone." Both of us break out laughing. I wish she'd find a hot boyfriend and share with me the joy of sex on Sundays. And Mondays.

The wind is blowing hard, picking up dust and debris and the piles of leaves we raked. What a waste of time. They swirl along the ground in a colorful dance, snubbing their noses at me. Ph...plph...swsh.

My life is torn between lust and politics. Both are equally frustrating. There was a short mention in the news of tens or hundreds of thousands of bred and stolen Lebensborn babies. Next day, nothing. A shot in the dark, silence. The blonde babies unhappened. But something starts gnawing in me. And it has to do with the babies. At night, they steal into my dreams again, their faceless, colorless shadows sitting on newspapers, locked in cages with carrots.

Last night, they began to glow. Wet paint in lurid colors came seeping from their eyes dripping down their bodies and over my hands. The burning hot paint woke me up from a powerful dream, a vision etched into my mind and burned into my hands. I wish you could get your own hands wet and feel my horror.

The gnawing thought is getting clearer with every dream. It lives on top of my brain like a word on the tip of my tongue.

Meanwhile, Gernot and Irene finish each other's thoughts like old people. He, with his scratchy baritone, plays the guitar and sings love songs to her. If she only knew how he flatulates right after she leaves!

I enjoy my walks along the river with Frau Strauss. She swoops me up into her stories of life, history and religion, the impact of small actions leading to catastrophic ones while we sit still with blinders over our eyes. Like my teachers, she does not delve into our recent history, never mentions the people she lost. Wounds are still raw. The scab might come off.

Sometimes I notice a slight change in my behavior when I am with her. I treat her with more deference than I treat others. Is it because she is Jewish? Because the two of them are the only ones left of their family? It doesn't seem right to either one of us if I act false for whatever reason. During our next walk I ask her how people react to her being Jewish.

"I wish things could just be normal. It might take years for people to feel comfortable again, and not just Jews. All of us. One day, we need to address what happened as neighbors, as a country. When the time is right."

"Tell me, am I trying too hard?"

"You do no such thing." She pats me on my back and hooks

her arm to mine. From then on, we walk arm in arm, and I treasure our friendship for years to come.

In the middle of the night, when the moon is bright, I wake up feeling at peace. The world is fickle and full of shit, but the shame is not mine. And I let go, feel it drain away and lighten my heart. What a burden I've carried. I bet those that should feel the shame most likely don't. Rats, the lot of them!

One far away day, Frau Strauss will introduce me to two Jewish students. I will see them simply for two guys with four eyes on me. The older wants to marry me, but the other will be my lover. By then I will have learned that ethnic killings happen at any given moment somewhere. There is good and ugly the world over. In between are the opportunists. No country is immune. For the next weeks, I feel good and proud to have a grip on life.

How little I know that life has its grip on me.

36

SECRETS

It happens the morning I wake up dripping in sweat, bolting out of bed in a panic. What's left of the nightmare are Gernot's four severed limbs with its huge hands and bare feet walking around in our yard in a desperate search for his family. Bile rises to my mouth from the shock. Gernot is not my brother. How could I have missed it all those years!

I take the steps down three at a time, crash against the wall, stub my toe. Who is he? Who are his parents and what are mine? Mutti and Vati are in the kitchen. One look at me and Mutti says

"You are white as a sheet, a freshly laundered one. Come here, sit down." She tries to sound cheerful.

"I saw only his large hands and feet in the yard."

Vati throws his head back and holds on to his few hairs.

"I am so sorry. We were ready to tell you. Ach! I guess your dream beat us to it."

"His bloody limbs walked around the yard without the body." I look at them wishing me wrong.

"So sorry," she whispers.

Vati calls it bad timing. "We are not Nazis, if that's what worries you. Let's talk about it tonight. Meanwhile, he is your brother just not by blood." He puts on his green leather coat, kisses my forehead, plants a quick peck on Mutti's slightly opened lips, and off he goes on his new and noisy scooter.

On the way to school I carry the heavy burden of my thoughts. They are heavier than my backpack and I cannot take them off. Even a boy, blinded by my most dazzling smile, couldn't carry them for me. Will I still have a brother? What if my family will never be the same again? I do what I often do, diving into the depth of my despair, an explorer of my own mind, and torment myself knowing it's fake. Of course, we'll be fine because nothing will change.

In the evening, I pick through the Sauerkraut and lick around my sausage so no one else will eat it, I hope. Everybody is jabbering. About the stupid experts and their poor advice to keep Gernot's secret until I turn eighteen. Gernot and Ulla yelling they wanted me to know the truth since my birth.

Adds Ulla, "and you blew bubbles with your saliva and you were so cute, and it would have been the best time to tell you."

"We should have listened to Gernot and Ulla, that's for sure," says Mutti as we mosey over to the living room.

"Bad timing," says Vati again. "Ach. My youngest brother got brainwashed in the Hitler youth and later got one of the stolen baby boys from a Lebensborn home. When his wife died shortly after, he didn't want him, and he brought him to us. The one good thing he did. We adopted you, Gernot right after the war."

"It was love at first sight," says Mutti. "I had a miscarriage and you came at the right time, my dear. But we never forgot that you were stolen at two years of age from parents that loved you, and endured two miserable years at a home. Tell Sabine about it, Gernot."

"First tell me, are you my brother or not? How does that work?"

"You are still my little sister. Hilarious, annoying...."

"Well then. Might as well be my brother. I couldn't marry you even if I could. You'd be too ugly, old donkey."

We spend the rest of the long evening talking and eating chocolate candies filled with liquor. There's an electricity in the air, or maybe it's the liquor. My limbs feel like they could walk around on their own like Gernot's but more fun.

The clock strikes twelve. Midnight. Its rich, resonating sounds taste of dark chocolate. Gernot is conjuring up early memories of the home. He seems more serious than I have ever seen him. Maybe being in medical school is changing him. He sounds smart like a professor.

"Kids spoke many different languages, but we couldn't use them. We had to speak German which we had not learned. It was like being deaf and mute, an appalling loneliness, isolated without walls. If we disobeyed, we got spanked. They ripped our family, culture and language right out of us. I remember howling screams and an eerie quiet. I withdrew into my own little me and found refuge in my early memories. But slowly, they faded away as we learned German and were taught songs and played games. Then there is a gaping hole of something that happened, a feeling in my stomach that there was a 'thing.' It made leaving the home harder than the misery of being there."

"So you remember a 'thing' without a clue to what it could be? How can you remember something you can't remember?" I ask.

"I don't know. It's weird. Yet, here it is... a 'thing,' stuck in my mind, waiting to be solved.

"Do you remember anything from before the home?" I wonder.

"I do from my earliest years. A strange memory that surfaced many years later when I ate my first peach. Besides making a big mess - do you remember, Mutti? - I saw myself sitting in the dirt, chickens nearby, in a sunny, arid landscape with strange scraggly trees. I was eating this sweet fruit amidst lots of people and animals barking, yelling, baying. It's a strong image to this day."

"You spend much time in your room. Is it to be alone?" I ask.

"No, I don't like to be alone, I just study a lot. It's good to hear all of you, including your high notes, Sabine. And I don't mind your visits even though your dicey questions about boys give me heartburn! I also wonder about my other parents. Are they still alive? Do they miss me? And why do I so strongly feel the void of 'the thing?'"

. . .

"How did they breed so many babies?" I can't imagine.

"Soldiers raped," Vati looks at me - "that means using force - or they had affairs with local girls. Then the babies were taken. Like sowing and harvesting a crop! Hitler loved the Norwegians the most for their blondness. Our blonde soldiers were likely asked to make as many babies as possible in all of the occupied countries. And probably, they just stole them. We really have no way of knowing."

"His memory does not match a Norwegian landscape," says Ulla. "We might find his parents in a sunny country."

"Those filthy bastards do not want us to find anybody. They will wait till they rot in hell in their own stench." Mutti's anger is visceral, raw, and now I understand why.

Vati gets up and stretches, walks to the window and stares behind the curtain. It's one in the morning. The world sleeps, the night is dark as the devil. A dense dark without stars or moon or any lights. What does he see when he stares into such impenetrable blackness? Are his own thoughts reflecting back to him the way the river roars back at me? He turns around and speaks.

"There are rumors of whole villages bringing their children to town to be vaccinated. They came in buses, on bikes, in carts and carriages for their kids' sake. Then the blondest and health-iest ones were taken. If people complained? Loud voices were silenced. Another word for murder."

Gernot shakes his head with a bit of a laugh. "I sure won't join the German Aryan elite to make Germany whiter again. Irene and I will try for crispy brown babies."

. . .

The box with the liquor filled chocolates is nearly empty. Ulla is picking her cuticles. Our eyes are glazed over from fatigue, and we go to bed.

A few days later, at school.

Two men escort our principal out the door.

What did he do? 'Crimes to humanity.'

What crimes? We never learn.

He was the best teacher I ever had. How will I make sense of it? How will I square his evil with his wisdom and his dark side with the light he shone?

I can't and feel shivers.

After school, Werner is waiting at the corner. He gives me different shivers, looking so distressingly handsome. I slow down. We don't speak but gawk, awkwardly, sniff around each other like puppies, and I remember Gernot's advice to think with the brain in my head, not the one in my underwear or something like it, and I pick up my pace, feeling his gaze follow me and undress my backside.

It happens more and more frequently, getting looks that seem to undress me. I don't really like it, but I also don't mind, just not from the front. There is too much private stuff there, and they are finally rising like puff pastry.

I still don't have people to talk to, compare feelings with. Hannelore is my 'how to do it' person. That is not enough now.

I hunger to hear about the jingles in my heart, about the vibes that wrap around my whole existence over a pretty face, and the juices that flow so freely.

37

LOVE STRUCK IN SPAIN 1958

S nowbells and the first daffodils and crocuses stick out their heads in white and blue and yellow, and branches turn red with sap. A branch of lilac in a simple glass vase on our white tablecloth scatters the scent of spring.

After our simple evening meal of bread, cheese and salad, Vati announces a surprise. His green eyes glow like a cat. Ulla guesses he found a concubine, Mutti worries he found Jesus and lost his mind.

"How about we take the same trip I took on my bike in 1930, through France and Spain. This time in a car."

We are speechless. Then we scream. Are we really going to Spain? We are and I wish time would fly. After our cleanup, Mutti plays Chinese checkers with me 'to help it fly.'

. . .

There is a new bra in town. Several of the older girls wear it and their boobs look like sugar cones, pointy and perky. I would like mine to look like it when we're in Spain.

"What do you think of those?" I ask Mutti.

"You mean you want me to buy you one." Her brows are touching, her eyes squinting. "No way."

Gernot entered, glowing from a walk with Irene. "If I were your boyfriend, such a bra would have to come off at once," he says. Mutti, still trying to protect my virtue, goes 'tststs, Gernot!'

You guessed it! I don't get sugar cones. But most nights, Mutti plays Chinese checkers with me, and winter flies by as if it skidded on its own ice. Over the winter we got our first telephone, a real washing machine with a spinner, and a small refrigerator. At school, my pink poodle underwear was a big hit, even with the boys. There was nothing sexual about it, I think as I showed off the spider over the butt crack, and we all laughed.

Vati bought an old green VW beetle with two tiny windows in the back, and Gernot, Vati, Ulla and I take off. Irene went to England and Mutti invited Oma.

Mostly we stay off the Autobahn, winding instead through picturesque towns filled with history and cathedrals. I am humbled by their beauty, understand how one can find religion inside such wondrous places, but also smell the fear in every dark corner where the horrors of history are stuffed away and buried. We call them dead, but they live on, unseen, in crypts and in the silence. An eerie sound sends strange vibrations through me and each time, I feel glad to be back in the sun.

. . .

When we arrive in Lloret de Mar on the Costa Brava, a small fishing village, we put up our tents in the campground near the beach. At once, the neighbor's tent empties out its cargo: three hot students from Madrid drawn by our female voices. Two engineers, Pedro, Miguel and Luis, a student of medicine. And one single look at the latter strikes my heart with a lightning bolt so terrifying that I will be his forever. I blush, is all I can do.

Later, at the water faucet, he whose name is Luis, gazes at me with keen grey eyes. I want to taste his crisp body the color of honey, feel his sun-bleached hair, touch his strong-willed chin and be kissed. He has succulent lips. Our eyes keep their stare, filled with a new fierce hunger. I am love struck! Ready to mate if only we were animals. What a huge flaw of nature. I want him now and all over me.

At night, I dream of my eternal love, decide to give his name to my first born, Luis. Luisa if it's a girl. Night and day, I hunger for him. The days are of a deep sapphire, the hot sun baking everybody in its path to brown or ruby red, and clothing is skimpy. I smell him. He smells ripe and right and his pungent sweat matches my own. We spend our days in the water, on the sand or high up on a rock. I want to bump into him but am too shy to touch. Want to be naked but hide beneath my towel.

One night, Vati says: "Fine, you girls can go out with them, but Ulla, you stay close to Sabine."

I didn't know they had asked. I try to stay next to Ulla, but Luis takes my hand. We go dancing and he holds me close. I smell his neck. It makes my legs hang down like two limp celery sticks and I step on his feet. I can't even dance. Love is eating me alive.

We walk on the beach under a moonlit sky and sit down onto the cool sand, away from lights. Pedro and Miguel are flirting with Ulla whose skill at chaperoning is second to all. Luis pulls me on top of him behind her back. We are as close as bacon wrapped inside a roulade (a very thin piece of beef rolled up with bacon and mustard). He pulls my head towards his lips, plants the other hand on my butt and I turn into a flower in full bloom, ready for this nectar sucking male. We are lips to lips. I feel his tongue, worry to get pregnant and move my head by the width of two fingers. Move them right back. But his hot lips got cold feet. He does not try again. I am misery incarnate.

Much later, I think his kiss might have started the mother of all begetting. We will never know, will we?

Back home I suffer, pine for him day and night. He inhabits me, has crawled inside of me, yet leaves me with an emptiness I never knew. Love is cruel, and I am lost in these new feelings. We can cry away sadness and yell away our anger. This is different. I whisper his name with all of love's glory and agony. An image of the burning bush of the bible appears, suddenly clear in its meaning. My bush is burning like a grass fire and I touch myself, smell my scent, needing to know the very essence of me, of who I am.

. . .

One night I dream that we kiss. His tongue tastes of a lemony lollipop. He pulls down my bathing suit and we sink onto his sleeping bag, both naked, when Vati pops in ogling us. I wake up mad. It was only a dream. Couldn't he have let us finish!

I start learning Spanish, memorize a page of 'Don Quixote' just in case he comes and carries me off to feast on. He writes beautiful love letters in English, calls me his iceberg, and that he wants to melt me. But how can I write back? There exists no language to describe my longings, and I who is not shy am too shy.

There comes the day when pain finds humor. Ulla is most helpful and loving during this time. She makes me laugh with stupid songs like 'I love you so much, from head to your crotch.' And so it goes.

After a few weeks, I laughed my pain right out of my heart.

38

OH OH, WHAT'S HAPPENING

Dreaming of Luis turns my job of dusting into a most erotic endeavor. I rub and polish every corner of every room with a fervor as if it were him. I try to make him stay alive and not become dusty and invisible. Sometimes I rub hard because I am mad. He should have tried to kiss me again. Lips are for kissing. Nobody has tried lately, and there is an empty space in my heart, waiting to be filled.

Having found, and lost, my true love is life altering. It expanded the scale of my feelings, set the standard of what love should feel like. I often go alone on long bike rides to quietly stew in my sorrow love life rather than be with friends. The Rhein in its ever-changing beauty and power, its long colorful barges sliding downstream, is just right for stewing. It shrivels me to a size utterly negligible in the big scheme of things. The long road along its shore allows no cars and I am the only one riding my bike on this cloudy afternoon, clearing my mind of the last of love's cobwebs.

. . .

It feels very good. Darn, it feels good. I keep pedaling, and as I pedal innocently along, I realize that the good feeling is right where I am sitting on the seat. I keep going and going, and it feels better and better, like there's a bubble forming that's about to boil and burst. Then, a fiery earthquake rattles and jolts my privates. I stop and get off the bike; hold still to listen to my body. What happened? I don't know, only that it was very good. I sit down on a bench. Will there be more? Is it normal? And what is its name? It must have a name!

I stare at my bike. My bike, my first lover!!! My old rusty bike!!

At home, there is nobody to talk to. How can I tell them how good it felt? And now, I see so many possible lovers, most of them way better than my bike.

A student of Psychology asks me out, and again. He talks a lot to show how smart he is. German men like to do that. At times, he sounds smarter when he shuts up. His kisses and his words ignite no fire and I feel safe.

One day, he takes me upstairs to his apartment, carries me over the threshold and puts me on his bed. He does this and he does that, caressing while unbuttoning, and then some more, down to a whole new world of slutty. He is sly, knows his way around. I am reluctant. His body is skinny and too white, a 'plucked chicken,' is what I call those.' But more and more strong feelings stun me into a hot corpse with a most willing body. He is straddling me, and his tongue is nearly gagging me, the warm breath of his nostrils in my face. Snot air. I don't like it. Then, right then his soft and loving whispers reach my brain, the words still ringing in my ear:

"Don't worry, if you get pregnant, I'll marry you."

I tear away in panic, grab my clothes, bolt out of there and run downstairs, his voice following like toilet tissue stuck in one's underwear and trailing behind. I put on shirt and skirt and shoes before reaching the street. Never mind about the rest.

Am I a virgin or a slut? I could be pregnant now and didn't even enjoy it. What a waste it would be of my dreams of passion. Over the next few hours and days, I relive the moment and believe that he was not inside of me. I would know, wouldn't I? I am a slutty virgin is all. When I get my period, I am glad for both of us. He'd be stuck with a most miserable, cantankerous wife, and I with a lukewarm husband in need of lovers or a better bike.

I do remember him naked and that thing looking at me like a snake. I am a bit shy to ask Gernot, but I do.

"Gernot, do all naked men look alike? It's for reasons of learning," I promise. "And you almost being a doctor..."

"They are either circumcised or not, and either erect or floppy. It's good that you ask. Everybody should learn that stuff." I thank him and leave, wondering what circumcised means and why the hell didn't I ask?

Now I go out with boys from my class. We share the same level of innocence and stupidity. We party in Ulrich's basement on Saturday nights, dance and rock and flirt to a poster of Elvis and records of the newest music, Rock 'n Roll, and our juices and desires flow and grow with each swinging of the hips. We are a hotbed of weeds ready to bolt into bloom and multiply into the neighbor's yard except, we are all just good friends.

Until they get a bit older, a bit bolder, when the lights dim and we're close and dance with our arms around each other, those darn little boys, I feel them grow into men and into me.

At night, I have a dream. Sandaled and bare legged, I walk through high grasses on a breezy summer's day. The grasses are a golden hue with feathery seed heads, and they tickle my legs. As the wind whips up my skirt higher and higher above me, the feathery grasses find their way into my most sacred self. I wear no underwear. The wind blew it away and I see it float over the hilly landscape, followed by my colorful red and yellow striped top. I am naked but for my whipped-up skirt. The feathery grasses are starting to caress me, turning into burning fingers as I wake up in a puddle of my own lust.

My virtual sexuality gets sorely challenged when the two brothers enter my life again. You do remember them? They used to be the objects of my longings until they changed schools. The Gruber brothers, those naughty young men, are back. Once I ran into Werner last year. Or has it been longer? I see them at a street corner. It's always the same corner. It must be me they are waiting for. Should I turn around? I don't.

They are even better looking now. The older one, Robert, has Marlon Brando's rustic and tough looks. He checks me out like a man's merchandise, maybe a screwdriver, and makes me feel strangely willing right on the sidewalk. Werner is refined look-ing, a Cary Grant. We lock eyes, and I want to melt into him, feast on his handsome face. But I do neither. Am older now.

. . .

"It's been a long time." My voice is calm or trying to be.

Robert asks me to go to a party at some girl's apartment. "Her mother works full time and we are alone." His challenging look, the lifting of just one eyebrow, holy shit. Werner, usually the quiet one, says

"A bunch of us go there and, you know, we do whatever comes up."

He is talking about a stiffy and I get aroused. And he looks at me as my face turns a ruby red from thinking about both their stiffies.

"I'll think about it." I walk away. Holy shit. What's a girl to do with two of them?

I my dream that night I get stuck in a tangle of limbs, brown and white ones, hairy and smooth and shapes of all kinds, and one foot with a sock still dangling on its toe. There are legs any which way. It is a dream about the afternooner parties I get invited to but never go. I wonder why I never go. Is it my parent's trust? They often say they trust me. It's a damn burden is what it is. Trust is their weapon! I am wearing a virtual chastity belt, a cheap one since it doesn't always work. But there is also a strong sense of gratefulness, I must admit.

At home, I knock and enter Gernot's room. He is slouching on his bed holding a big fat textbook. Anatomy and Physiology.

"Hi Doc," I say, "do you have a moment? please I need your advice!"

He moves over and I sit down.

"Gernot, I am scared to get pregnant. Can you give me ANY advice besides squeezing a stupid pillow between my knees?"

"Really, at your age?" He looks at my stomach as if I were about to hatch an egg.

"Please! You were young once."

"Look, obviously, you can't get pregnant while you are menstruating."

"I didn't know! Thank you. That helps."

"No, please! Don't go humping like a horny rabbit. There are diseases and strong emotions. Remember my old advice. All boys are bad boys, and use the brain in your head, not the one in your panties. Sorry."

"I don't wear underwear. They are in the way."

"Holy Cow, girl, I mean Good God, are you serious?" He is leaning onto his elbow and looks straight at me, worried.

"Of course not, Doctor! I always wear underwear. I'd wear a tight girdle if I had one. You are right, all boys are bad boys."

I appreciate his information. I can't get pregnant while bleeding, and maybe a day before and after would still work? Maybe two days? Even three?

39

DEATH AND BIRTH

She looks like shit, her eyes puffy and red around the rim. She has been gaining weight around her middle and her black roots are way beyond their bleaching date. She gives me a quick 'hello,' sits down and I ask her what the matter is. She keeps staring at nothing, then finally whispers "My brother left us," tears streaming down her cheeks. "Mother cries all day."

"I am sorry." I pass her my handkerchief and wonder how it would feel if Gernot left us.

"Rudi couldn't wait to leave. He is old enough now. He hates Father, had to salute him in the morning, call him 'Sir.' They never saw eye to eye no matter what. But to be fair, on our birthday and on Christmas, Father gives us a generous amount of money, his hand on our shoulders, and he looks right at us. He is a general, tough and disciplined, but a good man."

"He is an ass. And probably a Nazi, making you bleach your hair. I think you would look better with brown hair. And my Father hugs me every day and in between."

"I am the ugly one. Rudi is tall and athletic, and his hair is blonde the way he wished mine were." She invites me to her home again, and I finally agree IF her Father is away.

It's a long bike ride through the busy city center to where she lives. Her Mother greets me warmly and feeds us a nice lentil soup with sausage. We have little to say so I say how much I like lentils with sausage, and she refills my bowl. And again. Then her Mother sends me home, in a rush to bleach Sieglinde's hair before her Father returns from a trip, or maybe I ate too many lentils.

"I'd rather not bleach it," her Mother complains. "It's so tough on her scalp."

As I am ready to leave, her Father opens the door. He looks down at me from high up with an excessively pumped up chest. His hair is bleached the same color as Sieglinde's.

"General Lange." He clicks his heels together.

"Sabine," I say, and he grabs my hand before I can hide it and squeezes it so hard, I hear my bones crack.

"That hurt," I yell, "ahhh, that really hurt." I am crying from pain, cradling and massaging my right hand with my left, the look of his cold grey eyes rather amused. From the top of my voice I shout "Asshole" while smashing the door in his face. It feels good!

At home I tell them about my day.

"He what?" asks Vati. "Bleached hair? He thinks fake blonde hair qualifies him as an Aryan. That's what I deal with at work. You understand why I can't salute these morons."

Mutti pats his hand a few times to calm him down, like 'nice kitty,' while I imagine Vati with bleached hair. He looks ridiculous but gets a promotion!

Knowing Vati's temper, I keep to myself how badly the Aryan ass hurt my hand. It's not worth his while fighting a general. For the first time, I feel how frustrating it must be.

The next day in class I feel strangely responsible for Sieglinde. Poor thing, with such a Father! She is like an old spinster is what she is with less sense of humor than a good corpse. And what better way to introduce her to life but to talk her into ballet lessons with me.

It is immediately obvious that neither one of us will ever be a dancer. My body seems good enough for everyday use but not as a ballerina. It takes long slender limbs like branches of a willow tree, to turn music into dance. Hers are short and plump, almost stunted, and the rest of her body has grown into big, soft landscapes featuring an awesome rump. But she takes to dancing with a blind fury. Soon, she wears a tutu and point shoes, comes to the studio every day and becomes quite good. But the better she gets, the more her lack of gracefulness turns her into a caricature. Not funny but sadly, she looks like a flying pig.

Next, she thinks of becoming a ballerina and I worry about her. Does she know the absurdity of it? But I keep quiet. Don't know how to handle it and am too lazy to ask Mutti or Ulla for advice.

One day, the day she realizes that it's not her weight but the structure of her body that cannot be changed, she throws herself off a high roof. And that's all I know.

It is incomprehensible. Adults say we can do anything if we

try hard enough, but I think we also need the truth. Adults need to tell us the truth without holding us back. What else could she have done besides dying? How about living? She could have kept dancing as a hobby, become a ballet teacher, sewn tutus, or be in the audience. Performers need an audience. Life is full of symbiotic relationships. One never needs to give up what one loves, we need to adjust. If I can't sing opera on stage, I can sing very high and loud in our kitchen for our neighbor's pleasure.

The next morning at breakfast we read in the newspaper that Sieglinde fell into a large pile of manure and is quite alive and, I bet she stinks. However, she is in the hospital with two broken arms and for observation. It is a dramatic event. I need to visit her but dread it.

"I want to say I'm sorry, and I want to call her a dumb cow," I tell Mutti.

"Don't say anything. Sit with her. Hold her hand. That's all she needs."

After school, I ride my bike to the hospital, ask for her room and wait for the elevator. When it slowly opens, Gernot is about to leave.

"Look at you! Why did you cut your hair? And what's with the new clothes?"

He stares at me. "I don't know you. I wouldn't mind knowing you."

"Gernot. Did they ... What the hell? Stop!"

He is walking away with huge feet. I run after him. He turns around.

"My name is Rudolf, I was visiting my sister and I do not know you." He slips out the front door.

I catch up and grab him by the sleeve, grab him hard.

"You are her brother from Heidelberg, and I have your brother. He is my brother. Same huge feet." I can hardly talk. "I am not crazy! My brother, he looks like you, identical, I thought he'd cut his curls." I grab both his arms and am almost nose to nose with this stranger whom I know so well. "Listen to me, please listen," I yell while shaking him, trying to awaken him to the news. Then I let go.

He does not move, looks like a mask with hands suspended in mid-air, and all ten chewed-to- a-stub fingernails are pointing at me, nasty looking creatures. This guy got problems! He is holding his breath and keeps staring at me. Then he plops onto the ground, a small grassy area at the exit. 'Keep off' says the sign. But he can't sit still. He is choking from the news and his emotions, gets up again, does a little dance as if needing to pee, then sits down again, lowers his head into his hands. And finally, his shoulders heave with heavy sobs. I sit down close to him and wait.

"I grew up in a home. One day, they took the only thing I had left in my life, my brother." He is shaking now from the shock and the goosebumps and I put my arms around him.

At the corner is a phone booth. "Don't go away," I say, "I'll call my Father, he'll know what to do."

Ten minutes later, Vati drives up, brakes screeching, tires

leaving marks on the dirt which flies up against the car. He gets out, sees Gernot sitting on the grass and walks straight to him. One look, and he knows. Our Gernot has a brother. He sits down next to him in his good suit and smiles at Rudi.

"Yes," he says, "we have your twin brother. He missed you all these years!" Rudi starts to cry, and Vati's eyes are watery. "I'll call my wife. You guys go ahead on your bikes. We'll talk at home."

Vati runs to the phone booth and makes his call. It is quick. Mutti will be expecting us. Then he drives home, Rudi and I following on our bikes. When we get home and go up the two steps to our covered entry, we hear Ulla yell "they are here."

Her light footsteps approach the door, Mutti right behind her. They hug him, nearly eat him alive. Poor Rudi. I should have forewarned him, but he seems not to notice. He is looking over their heads for his brother. And when he sees him he tears through the ladies, then stops and for an instance they lock eyes, each seeing himself in the other, tall and robust, blonde curls cut short the one, kept long the other, same blue eyes, clear skin stretched over high cheekbones and a good sized manly nose. Now they hold on to each other with four huge hands, overcome by long lost memories. We go inside to give them space. After a while, we hear them quietly go upstairs. Their hearts are too full for food. So are ours. But we eat anyway.

· · ·

At night, I dream of bombs hitting, body parts flying, and Sieglinde wrapped into the Nazi flag, bloodied from butchering her father. I wake up in a cold sweat.

How could I have been so thoughtless? I mocked her dark roots, called her Father an asshole, then talked her into ballet lessons. Did I think I could 'fix' her? Or did I do it to please myself? I am not sure.

Breakfast is a quiet affair. Coffee, bread, butter and jam. Two young men with eye buggers and pillow hair, subdued and emptied of words after their long night of trying to untangle the web of their existence. Vati is thoughtful. Mutti and Ulla with a thousand questions in their eyes and as many unfinished hugs in their arms for that young man, but both are careful not to overwhelm.

"I'll call your Mother and ask her to join us." Vati is walking towards the hallway.

"Without my Father," Rudi yells after him.

Frau Lange arrives twenty minutes later. Our new twins wait in the dining room till we call them. She is out of breath from the bike ride, her grey hair stuck to her forehead and dark patches under her arms. She is big framed and concern over the call made her pedal too fast.

"Coffee for you?" asks Mutti.

"No, just tell me what's so urgent."

"We have a son, same exact age as Rudi," says Mutti. "Both were adopted from a Lebensborn home, and they have met. We would like you to meet them both."

"They have the same huge hands and feet," I add to get her prepared.

Frau Lange is not quite sure what to make of it.

"Ja, I guess."

There is not a dry eye when they enter. Frau Lange looks them over for a long time.

"Jesus and Maria. I'll be darned."

40

THE AFTERMATH

What now? Both young men are starting their second year of studying medicine. They are ecstatic to have found part of their real family. They are also smart and thoughtful. After seventeen years apart they might be too different to live together. Mutti invites him to stay with us any time he wants to.

Before Frau Lange leaves, she takes my hand. "Come along. Siegi was hoping to see you yesterday."

"I am so so sorry," I blurt out, "it's all my fault. I didn't mean to..."

"Shush. You're the best thing in her life next to Rudi and me. You saw her where others ignored her, you talked to her and came for a visit. The only girl who ever did."

"I called her Father an ass."

"He is an ass."

"But I knew ballet was wrong for her and still I talked her into it."

"Fiddle sticks. She knew. She wanted to be a ballerina as much as a fighter pilot. No talent for either. Her Father makes fun of her, crude and ugly fun about her body. That's what made her do it, and not the first time! You are good for her."

We ride our bikes to the hospital. I half expect a third brother to exit the elevator, but it's empty and we go up and find her room. Sieglinde has both arms in a cast and her puffy eyes are red. I remember Mutti's advice 'silence is worth many words,' and remain silent. It's not easy!

"Siegi, remember Rudi telling us he knew he had a brother? His most distinct memory from the home? The day they took him away and he had to stay behind, alone, our little boy with a broken heart and we could never fix it. Well, this phantom brother lives in Bad Godesberg."

Sieglinde is perking up. Her pale color got a feverish glow and her eyes are coming more alive than I've ever witnessed.

"He is my brother," I say, "they could have met a long time ago had I visited when you first asked me to."

"They might have never met. What matters is they met," says her Mother. "You are kind of like sisters now, sharing two brothers."

"But you can't do stupid stuff again. I felt guilty."

"I was a dumb cow and won't do it again. In the mirror I saw what you all saw. A pig on point shoes. I only blame my Father. He probably doesn't even care." Her tears are welling up. "When can I meet your brother? My other brother?"

"As soon as you are up to it, Siegi," says her Mother.

I touch her fingertips and leave.

. . .

Seldom do the days pass as fast as they pass in our minds. One hour ago, Rudi left for Heidelberg. Three days was all he stayed, the new brother, not enough to get to know him well, but well enough. Like Gernot he is insightful and intelligent. But his profound hate for his Father scares me. 'I might have killed him had I not left,' he said. 'The way he treats Mother and Siegi. I'll never forgive him.'

Rudi hopes he and Gernot can study together for the rest of medical school. Gernot is cautious.

"I suddenly have a brother! At night, I wake up, realize it's not a dream and burst into smiles. He filled in a big part of my story. Remember those scraggly trees in the sunny landscape with peaches? They are olive trees. They triggered Rudi's memory during a trip to Italy. But there is a dark side to him. Better not spoil it by living together. Besides, I'd never leave Irene."

From now on, Rudi visits every other weekend. It's too much. Our house is too small for a new brother like him, whose resemblance to Gernot is skin deep at best. Peel it off and find utter chaos, anger and deep-seated melancholy. I can't handle it and tell Gernot how much Rudi's visits distress me.

"It's hard on everybody. He is disturbed, a raging lunatic." Gernot gets up to stretch and he opens a window. An afternoon breeze is blowing over the Kottenforst and gently moves the curtains back and forth. He turns to me.

"Sometimes he faults me, FAULTS ME, for abandoning him when we were four years old! Other times he gets mad that I got the better deal with you guys. Reason doesn't work. I am glad to study at Bonn University, live here and be with Irene."

"Does Rudi know he is a Lebensborn child?"

"Of course. It's part of why he is so disturbed. Look at his fingernails, chewed to the bone, knowing that his adoptive Father is a Nazi. They carry the moral guilt for the theft of kids like us. And for the rape or murder of our real parents. Imagine that."

So much for my two brothers being the future Nazi elite of Germany.

41

DANGEROUS HORMONES 1959

Confusing thoughts and feelings are fighting over my unwanted virtue. At almost seventeen, all I want is hump like the cat we hear in our yard at night, but I don't.

Robert started University. Werner, the younger brother, has recently started to wait for me outside my school. He carries my heavy bag and walks me home. During the walk he has started kissing me on the cheek. Soon he was into my mouth, and today he pulled me behind a bush and kissed me while his hand moved under my top, held on to my nipple like I might run away, while trying to lift my skirt with the other, for heaven's sake, like a bull behind a bush in the middle of town! I stopped him. He carried my bag anyway. That's the kind of guy he is. Tonight, he will pick me up and take me out.

I rush home, charged with my own hormones. I sniff my underarms. They need washing. Sniff my underwear. Good enough. When the bell rings I am ready. Mutti opens the door. Werner enters and I come flying out of my room. Mutti looks at both of us, probingly. To him, to me and back again to him.

"What are you up to?" she asks, checking us one more time, very slowly.

"We are going out," says Werner.

"Sabine cannot go out, she is sick." My sweet Mother uttering such a lousy lie!

"I am not sick, and you know it."

"Yes, you are sick." She shuts me up with one single look. Then she turns to Werner.

"You must go home! Sabine cannot go out."

She hurries him out the door as if afraid we might start mating right under her nose. I am so baffled by this Mother of mine, I don't know what to say, but she sure does:

"He is a troubled young man with a handsome face, dangerous, out to seduce you, and that's all there is to it." Never has she talked to me like this. My fury dissipates. She is right. He and I, we would have for sure. I go in my room to sulk, wanted to be seduced so badly.

I could be pregnant now, couldn't I? One moment is all it takes. I should thank Mutti for saving me but have no intention of ever doing so, since she also spoiled it. I ache for Werner. And had Robert asked me, I'd ache for him.

From now on, Mutti wants to meet whoever it is I want to go out with. She never seems to like the ones my body craves: the naughty ones. Always the naughty ones. So now I don't even bother going out with those. It's a sad life!

· · ·

When I wake up, something new is in the air, an urgency to thoroughly live life, to gamble and take risks, to think and not be foolish, to get smart and be very slutty, all at the same time. From one day to the next, we enter adulthood and teachers address us with 'Herr' for men and 'Fräulein' for ladies. 'Fräulein Birkholz,' say the teachers, and 'Fräulein Sabine,' the neighbors. The age of making curtsies is over.

Werner is waiting at the corner. Our corner.

"Let's go to my place. I have a surprise for you." He grabs my bag under his arm and guides me with his other on my lower back towards his house. Robert opens the door. "Surprise," he says. Shit, is he the surprise? The three of us are standing in the small hallway with its grey linoleum floor, a hat rack and hooks for coats. We hear each other's pulses beat. They come a little closer. We will crash together in a tangle of limbs. I am leaning against the wall for support, try to use my brain which is braindead. All that's left are strong currents from three strong magnets. Werner is kissing me now, gently, and I respond to his full lips, while Robert pulls down my skirt, and nothing matters any longer. All I remember is a mattress on the floor, unmade, and the three of us in a fever, a good one.

At the end, we lie exhausted in our juices, gutted and smelly like well marinated fish, my belly lit with the soft glow of a candle. I don't ever want to move.

Plop, plop, plop. Heavy footsteps jolt us awake and apart, a fall from paradise straight onto earth, naked. Their manliness, ready for another round, shrinks into a pitiful wet noodle at the click of a key turning in the door. We jump up, embarrassed by our nakedness. They look at me in panic, thinking 'where can we hide her?' Nowhere. There is no closet. A small dresser, our shoes on the floor.

For one moment they look towards the window, two young boys afraid of their mother. Would they really toss me out? All the things one can think in one fleeting second! But the footsteps turn back down the stairs. The mother, there's something she forgot. I dress and leave, careful not to be seen, and exit through a hedge of hazelnut bushes that divide this apartment from another. Grab a couple of nuts to eat on the way home.

My legs walk as if on a rainbow. The reckoning will come soon enough. Mutti will have one look at me, worse, she'll sniff the strong double dose of sex. I stick my nose into my top to take another whiff of this ambrosia of lust. Will I ever find another lover and his brother? No. I remember the look on their faces, the look of fear, the look of little boys. They are not the men I thought they were. What was I thinking? And who, would I say, the thought hitting me like a hammer, would be the father? In a panic, I hope for twins. In our yard, Mutti is busy chatting with a neighbor and I rush upstairs to wash, twice, and look in the mirror. Who did I think I was? I am nothing but a young girl with a dumb smile on her face! Ach.

My period arrives hours later. Maybe I knew it was coming, but I don't think I considered it. I must keep it in mind from now on.

. . .

Once we taste the ambrosia of lust and life, it begs for more. My body is thirsting for it but not for them. I never go back. The look of fear on their faces is etched into my memory as is my own face: young girl with dumb smile.

I take a break from men, not easy when they stare at me with those hungry goo goo eyes. But then I find another lover without a brother and without a bother, because, he says, he can't get me pregnant. Something about chop chop, clip clip.

42

TURMOIL IN THE FLESH AND IN THE SOUL 1960

He is a dark haired, fiery eyed diplomat, smooth, knows how to work a girl. Knows which places to find and what to do there with sly fingers that don't ask but do and make me want. A fast worker, experienced, in my knickers before I know. 'Not to worry,' he says, 'I can't make babies, and 'not to worry,' he says, 'my wife had enough of me.' And he plays me like a grand piano and makes beautiful music in my body. 'Without you,' he says, 'I take to the bottle to drink away my sorrows. With you,' he says, 'I need no drink.' You are my Beatrice, my muse.' Yes, he is also a poet, but he sure is no Dante!

I don't love him. Never let him kiss me deeply with tongue and soul. After all, he is married, and I have high standards. It is strictly an arrangement where he pleasures me while I, in turn, listen to his poems. It makes him happy since his wife is not only tired of him but also of his poems. Then we talk. He is a true Roman Catholic, or as I see it a roaming Catholic, who tries to prove the existence of God to me while disobeying

God's command. I try talking sense to him with logic, history and my own thoughts. But to no avail. True believers believe no matter what because they must. Unquestioned belief is the cornerstone of religion and its biggest flaw.

We have our strange relationship all the way to the end of high school. He helps me resist other men, since I now have my very own lightning rod. And since he is Italian and likes pasta, I see that sex is like pasta. Hard till it's cooked, then it gets soft with a sauce on top.

About dark haired, fiery eyed diplomats. He helped me through the worst of my teenage years in a most pleasurable manner. What's bad about that? But after him, I never again indulged in encounters with married men, even if they threatened to take to the bottle. It doesn't seem right. I wouldn't like it for Mutti or Ulla or for me one day.

43

UPDATES AND BACKSIDES

If you don't know yet, Sieglinde and her Mother moved to Heidelberg to be near Rudi. Sieglinde won't need to bleach or curl her hair ever again. Towards the end, they got on my nerves so badly I was ready to throw all three off a high roof.

Gernot and Irene got engaged. They will move to Berlin, he to finish his studies, she to start University. Ulla met somebody at the University of Cologne. Most nights now, she stays with him instead of taking the train home. Can't blame her, but I'll be left alone with my parents.

A few days before Gernot's departure, we sit around with a glass of wine, a golden sunset streaming through our trees, my heart overflowing with melancholy.

"When did you know Irene was the one and only?" I ask Gernot.

"There was never any question about it. I saw, I conquered,

and I grabbed." He grabs her in jest but catches her empty sleeve and we laugh at him.

"How about you, Ulla? How long did it take you to know?"

"After a few hours with him it was as clear as chicken soup."

"That's not clear."

"Exactly. It was nourishing, invigorating, the whole world fell into bloom. The other suitors drained me of my life force."

Mutti laughs, "I am still not sure about Vati."

He admits that Mutti was six months pregnant before they wed.

"It was Oma's wrath that made me marry your Mother, not the fear of God as she claims."

"So how long did it take you, you know, to ah..?" I ask.

"By the time we were done walking up the steep ski slope, the snow started melting under our feet" says Mutti. "But don't worry, we didn't...."

"Not till the next day...." Vati chimes in. I guess he had a second glass of wine. Mutti isn't too happy. She would have liked to keep that a secret, being my role model and all. Not one morsel of wisdom from any of them!

"How will I recognize the right one when he shows up?"

"You might not. But he'll be smart enough to let you know," says Mutti.

It's time to say goodbye. Overnight, life changes into too quiet. Amazing how much noise and joy Ulla and Gernot contributed to our lives. Now I hear Vati turn the pages of his book. And when Mutti fills the house with passionate music, I hear the quiet waiting behind.

I miss them dreadfully. There was a lifelong comfort in knowing their thoughts, their laughs, their smells and habits. It won't ever be the same again. At least Ulla visits most weekends and we see her belly grow.

Finally, I think of things to do, dream of places to go. My time to leave will come soon enough. All I need is money. I start to tutor kids in math. As an upper classman, I qualify to go on trips with students from Bonn University for a pittance of the regular charge. And soon enough my pittance allows for an exotic trip during next summer. All I need to do is choose a country. Meanwhile...

44

MUSKELSCHWUND

He is slouching on a sofa, movie star handsome, with hair the color of an almost moonless night. He is whispering to a girl. When I see him a bit later still sitting in the same slouch, on the same couch, his dark eyes are pointing at me, feverish in their intensity and I move on uncomfortably, knowing that his eyes are following me. I am at a party with my friend Ulrike and ask her about him.

"He has a muscle wasting disease. From great athlete to barely walking in less than a year."

What a frightening future he must face with a fine mind and no body to hold it in. I would rather lose my mind and not notice my slowly decaying body.

It's been a few months since the party, and the young man has left my thoughts. I am sitting in the kitchen of a lady I need to talk to. She has to make a phone call and 'it will take a while,' she says. 'To make myself comfortable.'

. . .

I turn around at a low swishing sound and a squeaky door which starts to move and gets slowly pushed open. The young man with muscle loss slithers and squirms at a snail's pace into the kitchen. He can't get up any longer and lies on the floor in front of the refrigerator, a woeful wreckage of his former self. A deep anguish is spilling from his eyes, or is it an animal's fear of what's to come?

Before I know what to say, the young man asks me to sit next to him on the floor. His moist eyes dig into mine in a most cryptic way, as if pulling me down. 'Caution,' says my inner voice, but I lower myself close to him for lack of space. He begs me to please sit on him.

"You are my last hope to have sex with before I can't."

He tries to hold onto me with cold limp fingers that don't work well and repulse me, and I disentangle with ease, get up and sit back down in the chair. It is a horrible moment. An unforgettably horrible moment. Where for heaven's sake is his Mother?

He keeps imploring me with eyes dangerous as a well, easy to slide into. Emotions of every kind collide in my brain and heart. Empathy, anger, disgust and wanting to be kind. I feel used and sullied. Amidst this firestorm of feelings, I get up and leave, take my bike, walk out through the garden with its cabbages and fall flowers, my stomach churning and ready to puke out the disgust. How could he have asked me such a thing? For hours after I feel like a gutted fish. What would you have done? What would you have told me to do but leave?

Mutti says, "You can talk to me."

"I know. But I'll work it out."

45

KARNIVAL IN GERMANY

The older I am, the more life seems to be about sex. Putting on clothes just to take them off again. And then you get pregnant.

Ulla got married last week at three months pregnant. The proper sequence of things according to my family. 'Got to try out the plumbing first,' Vati likes to say, or 'don't buy the cat in the bag.' It was a simple civil ceremony. I stayed home since Ulla had nothing nice to wear and borrowed my only fancy green two piece corduroy dress. She barely fit in with her little baby bump. She looked lovely and very happy next to her new husband Bernhard.

There is a time in Germany when people get in touch with their inner barbarian. It is Fastnacht or Fasching, aka Karnival, the biggest festival in Germany, Austria and Switzerland, a time to seriously dress up and drink up before being pious for Lent. I decide to go to a University party with my friend, Ulrike, even though Mutti warns me.

"Dressing up means you are asking for it! Everything goes. The results usually show up nine months later."

Ulrike and I walk into a brightly lit hall with lots of chairs and mostly guys sitting on them in disguise, quite a few wrapped in sheets to look like sheiks. Someone grabs me, puts me on his lap, fondles my breasts and humps against me with what feels like a big boner. I can't get off him. Ulrike has been grabbed as well but got away, she is big and strong and helps pull me off. We go outside onto a large porch. It leads to the grounds, a large park with trees and no lights. Ulrike got snatched again and I am standing by myself. Another one comes and kisses me. Then he wants to pull me down into the park and I struggle. That's where it happens! There is probably at least one couple behind every tree!! I run back inside and look for Ulrike who is being dry humped. I hold onto her and he lets go. After all, there are enough others. We hurry to our bikes with a sigh of relief. What a bunch of drunken fools!

"Why do men think my tits are toys?" complains Ulrike.

"Because they are idiots."

We both know it's the size, enough to breastfeed an army.

By next year, lights will be installed throughout the park, illuminating every tree and corner. It was a bumper crop year for babies with unknown fathers.

46

FIRST EXOTIC TRIP - MOROCCO

What is one to do with extra cash from tutoring a kid in math and playing the flute at weddings but sign up for a trip to Morocco with a student group from Bonn University. It sounds exotic, it's a good deal, and I've never been there.

Vati and Mutti drive me to the train station in Bonn. I sit in the back checking my passport and ticket. Not checking really, just gazing and loving it. No way! The numbers must be wrong. Holy, holy shit! The departure time sneers at me: "I left an hour ago." There is no later train, no refund. The first thing I know to do is NOT tell Vati and Mutti. I check my wallet. I have only twenty marks. Double darn!

I kiss them goodbye in the car, rush inside and wait for them to leave. Then I get a taxi to the nearest Autobahn entry going south.

The driver tries to talk me out of hitchhiking, but I talked myself deeply into it, and he takes me to the start of my Moroccan adventure.

A car stops right away. A man opens the door. He looks sleazy and I wave him away, feeling very clever. Next, a large truck stops and I get in. It's too high to get a glimpse of the driver. But it feels right. A friendly older Frenchman and I spend the afternoon with easy chatter. My French flows well and I tell him I have a train to catch and a bus to find somewhere in the south of France. I forgot to bring the itinerary and do not remember the town's name. He is worried. "The south is big," he says.

In the middle of the night there's engine trouble. He flags down a large truck for me. Again, I don't know where to go except south. He is a nice guy and speeds up as much as he can and I appreciate it except in curves which he takes like a lousy lover, or maybe a good one if it weren't a road. I am getting just a bit nervous. Night turns to dawn and if I miss the bus, I must keep hitchhiking through Spain and beat my fellow travelers to the ferry in Gibraltar for the passage to Morocco. Finally, there is a sign 'Biarritz.' That's the name of the town!

At a fork, the truck driver flags down an old Peugeot. A friendly, newlywed teacher takes me the rest of the way into Biarritz. He wonders where to drop me off.

"No idea. How about at the first hotel in town?" He drops me of in front of a small hotel, then wishes me good luck. I immediately hear lots of German voices. They are eating breakfast. I enter the dining room and ask if they are heading to Morocco.

"Are you Sabine? How did you get here?" I tell them I hitchhiked all night and get a rousing reception and breakfast. It's a small fun group, animated and interesting.

Outside, my Peugeot is still waiting. I wave to him. He gets out and comes into the hotel, gives me a hug of relief and wishes me a safe life.

The rest of the trip is extraordinary. I started writing about it but better for you and easier for me if you head south through

Spain, then cross the water on a ferry, don't swim, and go see for yourself.

A short time after my return home, I hitch a ride. A nice man picks me up with a hand up my skirt before my butt is down, and when he stops at a light I jump out. Within a week, a woman hitchhiker is found cut into pieces; it's all over the news. 'What's the world coming to,' I think, and swear to never hitchhike again. My judgment of 'nice people' might be flawed.

47

A VICTIM OF THE WAR

We got a new math teacher. He is unlike any teacher I ever had with the eyes of a frightened animal and a body so thin a breeze might blow him away. He reminds me of the soldiers when they returned from the war, hungry and hopeless. Sparse but tightly knotted black curls dangle around his head and pencil sharp lips under a long aquiline nose have yellow debris stuck at the corners. It makes him look unkempt. I can imagine how handsome he might have been once, refined, with an aristocratic flair, but not now and he should not be in a classroom. He looks haunted and needs help.

Kids are cruel. Like rodents, they feel any weakness, sniff it out and attack. The boys take advantage of him, seem to suffer from urinary problems as they go back and forth to pee in an endless procession. I feel ashamed for them and sorry for the teacher.

One night, after about a week of him being our teacher, he waits for me around the corner of the ballet studio, leaning on his bike. There are no lights, I can barely see him but hear his quick breath through the darkness. "Fräulein Birkholz, you have stolen my heart and broken it."

What should I do? Go back to the studio? And how did he know I took ballet lessons? Making a quick decision, I wish him a good night and slip into the dark. He does not follow. At home, I tell my parents what happened, tell them he needs help. Mutti goes to school first thing in the morning. He never returns. It was a sobering and sad experience which haunts me for some time to come. But all I can do is hope that he gets the help he needs, this sad and lost man.

I believe he was a victim of the war, sent to work too early since teachers were badly needed. He might have been Jewish, quite likely from his looks, his colorful name, and his powerful fear. What if his entire family was murdered, he the only survivor? How can we attempt to understand?

48

MOIST AND HOT

Summer of 1962. My last summer before graduation. The time is ripe as a sweet summer's peach. I taste it on my tongue. A time far away to think about life. Time seems endless when it stands still, and we squander it, then try to catch it when it runs away. I want to live life to the fullest. A group of students is going to work in Israel at a Kibbutz in the Negev to atone for their parents' sins. My own burden of being German has long been lifted with the help of Jewish friends. I go for the adventure.

A massive earthquake struck in the Balkans days before we leave. The train tracks are cleaned up by the time we come through, but around us we witness a crooked world like towers of blocks built by a tiny child, ready to finish their collapse at the slightest breeze. Power poles lean at precarious angles. We quickly pass into the heart of the Balkans where our train slows down to pick up goats, chickens, cardboard boxes stuffed and piled high, the goats nibbling on anything and anybody. They also stink. We all stink, animals, people, the whole hot day stinks and my eyes sting from the smoke of people and the train.

A high wire fence and watch tower, ominous reminders of the political troubles, are near the two large tents that house our group at the kibbutz. We work alongside the older generation, mostly Ashkenazi Jews from all over Europe. Their amazing visions to turn the desert into an oasis, stone by stone, and their plans for desalination are deeply inspiring, since most of Israel looks like a desert, every hill covered by rocks.

"Your German is amazing," I say to the farmers who pick onions next to me.

"I was a physics professor in Berlin."

The other was a pediatrician. I don't ask the 'question.' Tragedies don't want to be dug up like onions. (Did your family die? All of them?) Being Jewish is like being German, you can't run away from it, you just are.

Our group is taking a trip to Jerusalem. At the wailing wall I stare into the old quarter at the orthodox Jews with their side curls and black clothes, women in wigs defying the punishing heat, all pregnant or with newborns and surrounded by kids of every age.

All the Jews I know are secular with a passion and open minded. They want one or two children, while these seem to mate at a young age and at high speed, holy Moses, bunnies all of them. With so many little ones they'll be spreading orthodoxy at an exponential rate. A disturbing thought that starts to bother me a great deal. What will this country become one day? For sure the opposite of what it envisioned. And once again, religion will be the culprit.

There is a law student in our group. He starts to hold my hand and fusses over me like a hen. There is a security in it, so I let him. With so many young and single guys and girls close together, hot from the desert heat and wrapped in a dense haze of hormones, it feels safe to look taken. He is interesting, lectures me about the law, presents situations and challenges my understanding. I like it a lot, am intrigued by laws and their flaws; a funny word, flaw, like a law with an expletive in front, f-law! Soon he wants to own more than my hand, but I keep him more or less at bay. On the last day, I finally agree to hitch-hike with him for the rest of the time.

Next day, almost boyfriend and I take off. Every car with room stops to pick up those in need, an unwritten rule in this new country with no crime yet. On the first day, we get to a town called Dimona, a tiny town with some very high buildings. What is hiding behind them?

"You can drop us off, please," boyfriend says to the driver.

"There's nothing here to see." His nails are filthy from scratching his oily hair. He seems reluctant to let us get out.

"We'll be fine," I say.

He shrugs his shoulders, grunts and lets us out. Boyfriend tells me about a supposedly secret nuclear power plant. We walk towards the buildings and for one split second, in disbelief, see a gigantic dome, a colossal round building, when two guys, late twenties, rush over to distract us, try to make unseen what we both saw. The Dimona plutonium nuclear research center, shrouded in secrecy.

They invite us to their apartment for a drink. I am sure their job is to make sure nobody snoops. Both are friendly, and one speaks German. Boyfriend asks if he may have a look around.

"I'll give you a tour, but there's nothing here, I wish there were. We could play pool."

And he and my lawyer leave me with the other one, who knows neither English nor French or German, and who is utterly too handsome to be left alone with. He is a striking, hunky, seductive specimen of a man. The room steams up the moment we are alone. We sit across a small table for two, ogling each other, two strangers with an animal attraction that is barely containable, a view into the bedroom and its large bed not helpful. He points to the shower to see if I want to take one. It has glass doors. Would he join me, soap me? Would he wrap a towel around me with his muscular arms? Touch me with his unshaven bristly chin, a bit disreputable looking but more tempting for it? I want to but shake my head.

The air is hot, moist, you can hear sparks ignite, and everything turns into an aphrodisiac. He gets me a glass of water. It dizzies me. Dark curly hair is covering his well-shaped head, a bit on his breast, how would it feel? I am going crazy with lust, imagine his mating sounds bouncing off the sides of mountains like thunder, bursting hymens and bringing new life. Am I deranged? Delirious? There weren't even any mountains that I remember. It's increasingly hard to sit in the chair without squirming like a horny cat on a blanket. I am my very own swamp.

I tightly squeeze my armpits to keep the pungent smell from escaping. He is looking at me and I blush. I want him, want him all around me, want to scream "what keeps you away? I'll be yours, even for a moment. No need to tell me your name."

I get up, stumble to the window. He comes close behind, his arms around me, his hands holding the window frame, and he looks over my right shoulder. I feel his breath and his hardness against my melting body. If I turn around, he will kiss me, and I'll be lost. But what if we miss our chance at total abandon to primordial lust? What if I have regrets? Could haves, should haves? My body is swollen with lust. It must be from the heat. I turn around. No, it is not the heat, it is the hunk.

We kiss as if we had been hungry for days, trying to find every crumb. He drops my skirt onto the floor, picks me up and I deeply inhale his scent as he carries me through the open door to the large bed. He is gentle the way he puts me onto the glossy wine-colored spread and takes off the rest of my clothes. My body twitches from his touches. He slips off his shirt. A strong and lean body. One moment later he is naked, opens a drawer and takes out a rubber, ties it with the ease of an expert and I arch my body toward him.

I never regret this encounter. Our paths were meant to cross and be remembered. The other two? They were playing pool. We used our time wisely. His name I never knew. But the feelings are still pulsating through me as I reminisce.

Germans are too well known to me, I believe, as I lean back in the old rusty car that picked us up next, me and my almost lover. How can I marry one? I might fall asleep during sex. I need somebody who rattles my whole being to bits and pieces.

. . .

We get dropped off in an Arabic town, Beersheba. Hot and thirsty, my armpits by now powerful enough to set off alarms. He stops at a door.

"Go in, get a drink, I want to check out a camera across the street." I enter a large, plain room with new hardwood floors, a wooden table and chairs in a bay window, otherwise stark empty. I sit down and wait for a waiter.

Men walk by outside, look at me, turn around, look again, then come inside. More men, same thing. Soon, I am sitting with five guys at my table. I show with my hands that I need a drink. I guess they are waiting also. They do sit a bit close, undeterred by my smell, maybe they like it the way men are. But still no menu and no waiter. How long does one wait for waiters, I wonder? But we are a happy little group and they are perfect gentlemen even though one of them gets up now, stands right behind me breathing down my neck. I don't like it.

Right then, a side door opens and a woman storms in. A highly vociferous and vituperous woman in her forties, hair bleached and made up with more color than care, mad as hell, as mad as only a very, very mad woman can be. She does not want to bring me a drink, I get that from the moment she enters with a high-pitched voice and no menu.

Boyfriend sticks his head in the door and waves me out. I leave quickly without good-bye, dying of thirst. My mouth is parched from the heat and all the earlier rutting. Outside, he takes my hand and says:

"You can tell your grandkids one day that their grandma was in a brothel."

He laughs. I stare at him in surprise, then crack up and join the laughter. No wonder I started feeling awkward in that room amongst those men without a waiter. What a funny moment. I keep cracking up, still in disbelief. Yes, I can't wait to tell my grandkids one day. Boyfriend takes my hand and we sit down at a café and order two huge glasses of lemonade.

Two days later. You see me now at the airport in Athens, not a crumb of food or a single penny to my name. The train station is on the other side of this sprawling hot metropolis and I'll miss the train unless I get a cab; I lower myself onto the floor and do what any respectable girl would do: I beg.

"Please..." I am holding out my hand. A young man, well dressed, in an obvious rush, stops his large highly polished shoes with a floral design.

"How much?"

"Five marks," I say, feeling like a hooker, a cheap one and quickly add:

"to get to the train station and buy some food."

"Here you go." He rushes on, his shoes a distinct memory but his face a blur.

Vati and Mutti pick me up from the station, a glint of moisture in their eyes. Mutti embraces me.

"My Sunshine. Good to have you home." Then she steps back. "Ooooh you stink."

Vati hugs me next. He can't stop smiling.

"You stink good."

. . .

I missed them too. Surprisingly much. I didn't notice till now. Their smiles, their happy chatter, feeling their arms around me, the scent of Mutti's subtle powder and Vati's scratchy chin, my goodness. I've taken them for granted all my life and I hug them all over again. They are the frame around my life, my rocks, my anchors, my lives' song. I want to hear all the news and the gossip. Gernot got a Fulbright scholarship to the US. and Irene will go with him. Rudi is not doing so well. He quit medical school and sits at home, depressed and rejecting help. Mutti and Vati planned a visit but he didn't want to see them. Back at the house, I can feel Ulla's baby kicking. A kick which will start a lifelong love for her little girl.

Dirty, hungry and happy, another week late to school. But I know that I'll graduate, even after their threats on Easter, when I spend an unexcused week in Rome; I feel it. When I arrive in the schoolyard during recess, when they see my face full of life and adventure, the principal and my headmaster shake their heads and then my hand, up and down, up and down. "Fräulein Birkholz," "Fräulein Birkholz" is all they say. But their smiles wish they could have done it too in their youth, feel alive, breathe in the world, find out who they are and what they are made of.

49

FINDING ADULTHOOD

L ike a piece of driftwood, life sweeps me to unknown shores. School is finished. I study music in Switzerland, but really, it's more the musicians, those men that peer into my eyes while making the cello sing, soft and sexy; I want to rip off my cotton dress and wear their velvety sounds. Baritones with voices that run up and down my spine make me shudder and melt whatever kept my spine upright. And the one who plays the clarinet with sounds smooth as drops of liquor on my lips. Ah! I drink in their touches, get seduced by their scents and lost in my life. All I know is how much I enjoy the floating, the freedom, the way men look at me like I'm a piece of pie.

One night, the cellist picks me up for a party. He looks like his instrument, well-fed around the middle with stringy hair on top. He takes me to a house, up the stairs, and up on a narrow ladder to the attic. When my eyes spill over the rim, it is crawling with naked bodies in all kinds of ways. Embarrassed, I go back down. The one quick look, holy cow, the things I saw and learned! But it leaves a slight after taste.

Slowly I start to feel my way into adulthood. I take more time to learn about a guy. How quickly it eliminates most. Handsome ones should never open their mouth unless they are also clever. Dull and dumb don't look so good. And I run from those that start their morning with whiskey.

There is a beauty in Switzerland that's almost too much to bear. When I sit on the old wooden bench on the hill above my room, under a sky that stretches high above the snowy beauty of the mountains, I breathe it in, softly and deeply. Often, I go alone to the beautiful old opera house, many stories high, and sit in the very highest seats with no gold or brocade, the pauper's section. Up there, amongst Italian guest workers who reek of garlic and ooze music out of every fiber of their being, it feels right that they sing or hum along, else their hearts might shatter. Once, I sang also. It felt like swimming naked.

Can you tell how lost I am? Why would I go to the opera by myself when someone would gladly join and buy me expensive tickets? For now, I find Swiss chocolate preferable to Swiss men, even though one of them is from Tunisia. In a sweeping decision I quit school, quit boyfriends and tell my parents not to send any more money. They deserve to spend it on themselves. All I need is a job. The rest will follow.

. . .

I am sitting on a bench near the lake, deep in my thoughts. A lady sits down next to me, mid-forties with an easy smile. We talk. She is from the US and invites me to a meeting that evening.

"There'll be food and nice people," she says.

I am suspicious and ask what it's about. And no, I won't go unless I know.

"You won't have heard about us. We are Mormons."

"It's a cult started by a con artist. Are you seriously trying to recruit me?"

She takes off without a word. She can preach but not listen. A cult takes away our freedom of thought. All religions do if we truly want to belong and not only go for the potlucks or to find a mate.

That night, a bit lonely, I stare at the letter on my desk, a blue aerogramme from a good friend of the family. Frau Strauss introduced him to me, a smart, handsome guy, funny, warm, gentle and well-to-do. He wants to marry me. A tempting moment in life, and I won't judge anybody for marrying a good friend and being happy. Maybe I am the stupid one. But there's no lust on my part. And love without lust is like a cake with no streusel. I need the streusel!

Thinking about streusel. I only ever want the streusel. What if streusel needs a cake?

Meanwhile, I am looking for a job at an employment office near the lake. The line of people winds down a tree lined path. A man in his mid 30s is sitting on a park bench. He is well dressed, his darkish glasses pointed at me. He is checking me out, then walks on over.

"You need a job, maybe I can help." He is very polite, the way the Swiss are.

"What do you have in mind?" I am polite also, even though he looks me up and down like he's about to buy a horse.

"I am with a group of professionals, doctors, lawyers, highly educated and very wealthy. They like to have parties, but often there are not enough girls. They would appreciate you."

"Why? What would I do?" Could he be a pimp?

"You'll get to know them, talk and dance, find someone you like."

I take a step to stay in line. He follows.

"These are high class guys, hardworking family men but you know, they like to have a bit of fun."

Do I look like a hooker? In crummy clothes and no make-up?

"And how much did you say?"

"It depends." He whispers, "You could make 100 Franks a night."

A whooping $823! I almost laugh out loud. Maybe it's time to start thinking more highly of myself. But I already do, kind of!

"I have had better offers," I say. Just not for one night. I sneer at him and walk off, wondering what his commission is. Pimp! Next I wonder how long it takes me to make $823. And I wonder at what point I'd agree to have sex for money, IF I liked the guy. And at what point if I didn't like him? One Million for a one-night stand? Ten Million? Virtue is not clear cut. You stay in a bad marriage for the money, don't you? In the moment, I am so deprived that I'd pay a guy for one good night, but it's just a thought. And I don't have the money.

. . .

And thus begins and ends my highly paid career as a hooker. I decide to leave my lousy Swiss love life and their chocolate behind. I will visit home and then, Munich, here I come!

50

BACK AT HOME

Our small kitchen is still painted red and white and its aromas are still the same, an integral part of feeling at home. The rhythm of my parents' soft accent brings about a lullaby of memories. It's where Ulla and I, for so many years, sang for our neighbor. Where she and I eviscerated the insides of a large cheesecake meant for company in my futile attempt at turning her into a bad girl.

She is visiting with her baby girl and Gernot and Irene are back from the US for a quick visit. They whisper when they hold the baby. I bet they plan on having their own soon! It's a vantage point in time, a dream before my eyes and happy memories for the future.

I ask Gernot about Rudi. He has been the only one in touch with him. He never responded to anybody else's letters.

"Rudi refuses help. I meant to visit but his Mother dissuaded me. 'It might make matters worse,' she wrote. He still bears me an obsessive and unreasonable grudge. He is at a point where HE needs to make a life or death decision. It has to come from him."

If I were Rudi, how would I see it? I take my bike and ride to the river. My beloved raging river with its powerful wisdom, if only one listens.

"Gernot," I tell him when I'm back, "if Rudi does not want you to visit, you must keep writing, otherwise he will feel abandoned by you a second time. Unreasonable or not, he was so little he couldn't understand that they took you. All he could feel is that you left. It's that feeling you must acknowledge loud and clear instead of explaining to him what he can't feel."

"That's kind of what Irene told me. Thank you. I need smart women around me!"

After a week, time is bossing me around with its annoying ticking of a cheaply made alarm clock. It is time to leave. Gernot and Irene, Ulla and the baby, we hug and kiss. Mutti, a bit teary eyed, and Vati, searching for a smile, take me to the station. Through the train's window I see them wave. They have adjusted to being alone rather than lonely. Now they are happy with us and different happy without.

51

THE BIRTH OF OUR SAVIOR

I t is the birth of our new savior, the birth control pill. Such splendid progress for womankind. My thanks go to Gernot who supplied me with this potent little pill before I left. All I need is a big potent man.

We used to be Goddesses before men grasped the significance of their quick but crucial part in procreation and turned us into chattel for a long dark time of suffering. Thank you, little pill. We women and our wombs are Goddesses again.

I live in Munich now, share a room with a violinist and study romance languages, still with no clue of what to do. I start to audit classes that offer more riveting subjects like, you'd never guess, the law.

On the side, I join the movie industry. If you don't sneeze at the wrong time, you can see me in "Jack of Diamonds" with George Hamilton and Zsa Zsa Gabor (1967), his 40th and worst movie. There are films that are only shown in certain theatres where I wear coconut shells and large feathers. When two TV commercials (cheese and shoes) are offered to me, I learn a new lesson. The offer comes with the expectation of favors on my part. I didn't see it coming and walk away, my inner Goddess a bit unhinged.

A nice part as the credit in a TV show makes up for it. It will be hugely successful and run for years, then more years with reruns. It is a short scene: I walk arm in arm with a young man in front of Munich's beautiful city hall when we find a dead body. Hundreds of spectators watch the filming behind ropes. I enjoy it, but not enough to consider being an actress.

I have a boyfriend. We are not a good match. He is a hawk, I am a dove. Lust without love doesn't work for me anymore and we split.

Gernot did visit Rudi after all during his short visit and before returning to the US. An emotional trip but well worth it. Rudi was seriously suicidal and hospitalized but is now asking for help. He enrolled again at medical school for the next semester, thinking of Psychiatry as his specialty.

"Wish him luck," writes Gernot, "he needs it! By the way, greetings from Frau Lange and Sieglinde who looks nice with straight shoulder length dark hair. She is going to dental school and dates an older guy."

52

THE LOVE OF MY LIFE

The large cafeteria inside the University is filled with noise, smoke and people on a mission. I sit in a corner, alone, watching them rush by. It's what I should be doing, rush and wait and waste another hour of my life in a boring lecture.

I notice a pair of eyes on me and look back at them for one moment. Oh God, I shouldn't have! He will walk over to me now and start talking, and with those eyes – I didn't even see the rest of him yet. How long has he been looking? Was I gross when I ate? Pick my teeth or scratch my boobs? He is coming close, carrying two bowls of ice cream. He sees me stare at the dark chocolaty one.

"You like chocolate, don't you?" He puts the bowl in front of me. "May I join you with my vanilla?" If there is one thing I cannot resist, it is anything to do with chocolate. And he, looking so chocolaty himself.

"Please do," I say, nearly losing control of my bodily functions. The second time we look at each other pierces me like lightning, the old precursor to an attraction with an animal's raw instinct. He is a mix of Omar Sharif and a snow leopard. What can I do but keep my cool and eat chocolate ice cream, maybe rub some on my face and arms?

"If I had stared at the vanilla, you would have said 'you like vanilla, don't you?'"

"Yes. I hoped you would. It is my first disappointment in you. I much prefer chocolate. We can split half and half?" He has a low, velvety voice, and shit, my body is already his.

"I'll keep my chocolate. You tried to impress me, it didn't work, sorry."

I act strong or he'll take me to bed within an hour. Maybe I can stretch it out a bit longer. Please, dear Jesus on a cloud, keep me grounded.

"You are worried. Why is that?"

"You are flirting with me. I don't know you."

"No. I am too chicken to flirt. But I give a cow for marriage."

"Holy cow. Which planet are you from?"

"Born in Egypt, pasture fed in Pennsylvania, educated at Stanford."

"What brought you to Bavaria?" He gazes at me with eyes dark and deep like the wild Sargasso Sea.

"Destiny. To meet you. You'd make an excellent lawyer. Not so good as a wife."

"I look forward to making the right man very miserable."

He reaches over and takes my hand for a handshake. He has elegant hands.

"I am Ali. And you are?"

"I am good."

"Good, would you like dinner with me tonight? About 6:00? I'll pick you up with my old bicycle."

He has an old bike like I do. I give him my address since we seem to share a similar bike.

Promptly at 6:00, nicely dressed, he arrives. There is a fancy car outside the door. I've never seen the likes of it. "Where is your bike?"

"In the car." He takes my arm, kisses my cheek and opens the door for me. There is a new shiny bike in the back. He must have just bought it.

"Brand new but it will get rusty soon in Bavaria," he says.

I sit down, a bit alarmed but he does make me laugh.

Our dinner lasts from 6:30 to 10:00. We eat slowly, laugh a lot and have serious discussions about every topic under the sun. We order several appetizers before the meal, then several desserts after, then coffee and more of it, then a drink to stretch our allotted table time. He is a passionate man filled with ideas about space exploration and technologies like harvesting the power of ocean waves and building satellites to eliminate the need for power cords in communication. He is a physicist and will be teaching here for one year before going back to California. I am nearly exploding from lust and from the food. He admits he saw me arrive on an old rusty bike and hoped it would help his courtship to own one himself.

We do not touch; when he takes me home, he barely grazes my cheeks with his. It would have consumed us right then and there. But I feel his lingering scent and dazzling brain throughout the next day and move in with him the day after.

"Which bed?" he asks, lifting one eyebrow. I point to the closer one.

"First this...." Animals, bloodthirsty animals. And our journey begins.

We live in a beautiful apartment in the city, our balcony over-looking a park and a small piece of the Alps. He has a cleaning lady and we eat out daily once or twice. He believes in using others for life's menial tasks so we can enjoy our time with afternoons of quick raw sex and long passionate nights. In between we study hard or cuddle and talk.

It is in the twilight hours, when day and night linger like lovers, a time that encourages thoughtfulness, that Ali and I talk about our families and our plans. He wants to take me to the US to meet them. I am not sure yet and ask for more time. He embodies everything I ever couldn't even imagine. His brain, his nakedness, his vulnerability of soul which he pours out like few men do, and his powerful touch that turns me into putty. Yes, he totally manipulates me. He pushes hard to change my mind about 'those damn lawyers'.

"Only bad lawyers are bad, and good lawyers are badly needed."

I believe him and sign up for law school. I study with vigor and get rewarded with high grades and his approval. If only I knew it was the right thing for ME!

He has more ideas. "Study international law, then you will be a big lawyer and travel many countries."

"May I still hitchhike? And backpack?" He thinks I must be kidding and laughs with his bright seductive smile and glorious teeth. I am kidding, but not entirely. It's the thought that matters to me.

There are more little things. He takes me clothes shopping and urges me to get a good haircut. It would be easy to enjoy if it weren't for his eyes, those eyes that see my imperfections and need to correct them. He picks expensive things, the way I never dreamt I would own or need. My old comfortable over the shoulder leather bag doesn't make the cut. I have to tear it from him.

"Don't you dare throw away my things, no matter how splotchy or smelly."

He grabs me and sticks his nose under my arms.

"I like smelly things." And I get all weak in the knees and he pulls me to the bedroom. And that's how we work things out.

I miss the mountains. We can see them from our balcony. I want to climb or go for long hikes. I beg him to come along. I might as well offer beef to a Hindu.

And this is my life right now. A fairytale which does not fit into the story of my life. But love trumps all and we are happy. He talks about kids and nannies while I climb high mountains and fall off a steep cliff with a scream. And the scream wakes me up, drenched in sweat, my heart beating like a drum set. More and more often the dream appears.

One day I tell him how scared I am of losing myself in his foreign world, how he needs to understand mine.

"Go hike with me, climb the mountains, breathe the fresh

air away from the city dust and wear old clothes if you own any.
The top of a high mountain will change you."

"Why is that?"

"It physically changes our view." He is not impressed but
buys expensive hiking boots. They remain in the closet.

"At least let's go on bike rides. You got a brand-new bike to
lure me."

"It served its purpose," he laughs. He is eight years older
than I, almost an old man and you can't change those.

When an agent asks me to audition for a one-hour TV special, I
say yes and get the part, filled with awe over such an unexpected windfall. Ali tries to talk me out of it. 'You'll miss too
many lectures, won't have enough study time.'

"I will get a law degree, but I don't aim to become a famous
lawyer or famous anything."

He is shocked. "But you are wasting your talent."

"You are wasting the little moments of life, those that
count, with too much ambition." Besides, I don't know what
talents he is talking about!

I call the agent, tell him to find another woman for the TV
show and regret it the moment he finds one.

We try, we really try, and things seem to improve. He comes on
short hikes with me and we get married, visit my parents for a
few days and Ulla. And I stop taking the pill and get pregnant.
His parents visit for a week, a long week. They are annoyed
that we didn't have a big wedding in California for their friends
and family from around the world. Ali craves their approval
and is annoyed that I can't pretend to be what they would like
me to be, walk around in high heels and dollied up just for their

visit. I am annoyed at all that annoyance. When they leave, things look up again. Every night, he checks my belly for the baby and when he feels its first kicks, he goes entirely crazy from love, and he books us a trip to Kenya over Easter vacation to celebrate.

It is a beach resort called 'Whispering Palms,' a rustic place far from humanity where coconuts hang high above private cabins, deadly missiles for unsuspecting heads, and there is one large dining hall for all guests. The rest is an empty beach, waves crashing against a coral reef some distance out, and jungle noises. It will be a heavenly week for the two of us.

We are walking along a pristine beach. Ali is bending his bare back to peek inside a low cave where the beach meets the jungle. I see a green Mamba slither above his brown back, a bright green blade of grass a hand width away, tongue drawn out with licking motions, ready to pounce and kill within five minutes. It is a sensationally intense moment that carries me to the edge of a new power: taking charge, calmly coaxing him out yet conveying the urgency without panic. When he is out of the cave, he watches the snake still searching for its meal. In a belated attack of nerves, when it sinks in how close he was to dying, he finds comfort in my arms.

But instead of quiet, idyllic days, Ali gets restless. He turns our time into a hectic week of nothingness, needs to fill life with more rather than less. I am disappointed when his eyes roam over the beautiful beach, the jungle, the coconut palms without seeing. He is already looking ahead to his work.

. . .

We are now on Safari. The camouflage of animals in the wild is spectacular and it takes a few hours to see them come alive. When they do, people go crazy behind their cameras, big bulky things with lenses that need constant adjustments in a frantic race to catch the moments. They are as fascinating to watch as the animals! Here, in the middle of Africa, with exotic creatures and high adventure; as when an angry elephant and once, a mad rhino run after us in our tattered old jeep that can barely make it through the deeply rutted dirt path. Yet here they are, safe behind a camera, watching it like a movie and missing life's very own pulse, Africa's heartbeat. Ali is one of them and I feel alone and lonely.

53

MY LITTLE BOY

We are back in town. Ali developed his photos and I admire them, don't tell him that he missed the most precious moments. He didn't get the Rhino!

My pregnancy is a happy one. We respond to each other early on. When the baby moves, I rub my belly and sing. Or I sing and rub, and he responds. Towards the end we are best buddies.

Two and a half weeks past the due date, I feel a sudden violent struggle inside of me, then, all movement stops. Petrified, I hurry to the doctor.

"Baby has a healthy heartbeat," she says in her white coat and grey hair. She advices not to induce, but to let nature decide.

Two days later I go into labor. The baby is stillborn, the umbilical cord tied around his neck. A strong and healthy boy who struggled hard to live.

My grief is bottomless. It hits me harder than anything in

my life ever. A tidal wave so powerful it unroots me, sucks the air out of my lungs and my whole being, and colors are no more. For a long time, my eyes will see the world in shades of grey and dark.

I am empty, filled with a love that has nowhere to go. It is an emptiness that fills its space with more emptiness. Sorrow needs no space. It wants silence, and it wants to scream.

Ali has his own grief, different from mine. He delves into work and leaves me behind, alone. Sometimes he goes out at night, alone. Or maybe not alone. Maybe he is trying to be there for me but doesn't know how to. Maybe he blames me somehow. Whatever it is or isn't, I feel abandoned and mourn him on top of our baby boy. And suddenly, I wonder what kind of a father he would be. Demanding? Expecting? Planning their lives without them in it? Love might not be enough to make a good parent.

After three months, he suggests we try for another baby. But I can't. Not again. I try to get back into my studies, but I can't. And sometimes, something makes me smile. And I know that life will be good again, I will be whole again. I cannot feel it, but I know and knowing helps. And I know that Ali will not be in this next chapter of my life and I cannot bear the thought.

It's an uphill struggle. At night, we hold on to our bodies, arms and legs wrapped around each other so hard it leaves marks, not wanting it to end.

During the day, we talk. Useless talk. I might want dogs one day and chickens. I don't but what if I do?

"We can make it," he says. "Love can conquer all, they say in the US."

"No. You need to find your ideal woman, not create her. The moment you recreate me, you will stop loving me because I won't be me. I don't mind wearing better clothes, get a better haircut, but your ambition for me is your own!"

"I know, my crazy woman. Crazy and wise." We stop talking and go back to the bedroom, as usual, and we stop talking about it altogether.

A letter from Gernot helps resolve our dilemma. Irene is pregnant and needs to take it easy for her last two months. Could I come and help, please?? Until her Mom can join?

Of course, I will. I take off the rest of the winter semester and make arrangements to leave for the US.

Ali and I are deeply, painfully sad. We cry in each other's arms. We were our one and only to each other yet neither can see a way out. He takes me to the train station for a quick, tearful goodbye. 'To let him know when to pick me up again' he says, but we know our last kisses will be the last.

I spend a few days in Bad Godesberg with my parents. I grieve hard, shed tears for my baby boy and plenty for Ali, and they grieve with me but wisely give no advice, only their love. Before I leave, Mutti hands me a little piece of paper with the phone number of her good friend, an opera singer in New York.

"Be sure to call her."

Ulla and Bernhard visit from Cologne with their baby girl. Just for the day. I want a family like hers, kids and a husband who loves ME, not a vision of me. Ulla is still the nurturing, kind sister she always was, and her presence is soothing.

. . .

Mutti and Vati take me to the train station for the trip to Luxembourg. It's where I'll board the plane to Iceland for the first leg of the long flight to New York. I see them wave through the train's window, their arms pretzeled around each other, and feel my cheeks get wet as both disappear around a curve.

54

FIRST IMPRESSIONS IN THE US

On the day of my arrival, I see a sign on a bathroom sink in Manhattan. It says 'For Whites Only.'

It is unexpected and makes me slightly nauseous.

Gernot picked me up and we quickly drive through the city into the fancy suburbs of New York with manicured lawns, manicured hands and as many manicured minds, I am sure of it. Ali would have liked us to live here! I would have painted fingernails and a team of gardeners instead of digging into the soil with bare hands and feeling the vibes of the earth and the wholeness one gets from touching nature.

How I miss him! It's a physical pain sharp as two knives twisting my insides. I imagine going back, being loved and ravished; and cornered. I concentrate on feeling the freedom, but it's not that easy.

. . .

Gernot's and Ulla's apartment is comfortable and cozy. There's a Picasso from his pink period and a painting by Miró, a dream-like fantasy for the coming baby to drool over. Gernot hired a once a week cleaning lady, and I am simply here 'for decoration'. They did not really need me, I needed them and am grateful. And slowly, I share my grief with them, heal from telling my story. And I learn by watching their love work. They accept rather than try to twist the other into new shapes. Any changes, I realize, must come from one's own volition, from the pleasure to want to please the other. They laugh with ease and like to touch and cuddle. One can live with that!

After a couple of months with Gernot and Ulla, the pain of the breakup has subsided. The pain of losing my baby boy is still terribly raw. It might take a lifetime. One morning, I am ready to venture out and surprise Mutti's friend, the opera singer, with a phone call. She invites me to join her for a matinee performance at the Metropolitan Opera house on the coming weekend.

55

AT THE METROPOLITAN OPERA

I wear my orange dress, the one I auditioned with in Munich. It brought me luck for getting the part and anguish for not accepting it. I use a tiny touch of lipstick since that's all the makeup I own. And off I go into the heart of Manhattan. Frau Graf will meet me at the Met. I arrive with enough time to admire the huge wall of stained glass in the entry hall designed by Marc Chagall, one of my very favorite painters.

She still looks the same. I was about seven the one time I saw her on a photograph. Beautiful with her dark hair, colored now, and lily-white skin with bright red lips. Few women had those at the time. How I loved those red lips and her high heels, and the notes she sang which seemed higher even than her heels. She laughs at my imaginary memories as we walk to find our seats.

Three young men look me over as we walk into our row, intelligent and hot looking hunks, all of them oozing a strong masculinity. They might be in their late twenties to early thir-ties. We sit right in front. One sits behind me and one seat over, and I feel his energy zoom into my left ear, getting me drenched in sweat and lust. I didn't have any for the last four months and am needy like a puppy wishing for a bone. What if he wanted a virgin? My mind starts to meander. I invent a new job in town, a hymen repair man who makes house calls. He looks like the guy who breathes into my ear, and he patches me up. Then I let him try out his repair since he guarantees his work. It's a vicious or a rather delicious circle of repairing and checking the repair.

When the music begins, I let it accompany my naughty thoughts. They complement each other and fill me with happi-ness. At the end of the performance, the three men approach us and he who has been studying my ear asks Frau Graf in the best of manners if he might talk to me, thinking she might be my mother.

"Hi, I am Stephen. What did you think of the performance?"

"So beautiful. My name is Sabine." We gaze into each other's eyes. I blush, feel bashful like a reborn virgin. I like him a lot! Elegant looking, on the rugged side.

"May I take you out sometime? Maybe for another opera, or dinner, or both?"

He lifts one eyebrow. Darn. That does it for me. I am sold. And in my very strong accent I say "I vould love sat. It vould be vonderful." Or we could just skip it.

He takes out a torn piece of paper and a blue pen and writes down my phone number. Then he asks 'The Question.' I didn't even know there would be one.

"Where are you from? I love your accent."

"From Germany."

Dead silence. Icicles had he breathed. Oh, why did he not ask first, before I felt those yummy feelings? Frau Graf tells him to call if he wants to, takes my arm and walks me away.

"He is Jewish and cannot bring a German girl into his family even if he wanted to. As soon as he said his name, I knew this would happen."

I am stunned. Here, in New York? Far away from the gates of hell? I was even liked in Israel, and Frau Strauss tried to marry me off to one or another of her Jewish friends' sons? They sure didn't mind, neither did their families. I don't get it. Discrimination. Racism. Intolerance. To me, there are no subtleties, it's all black and white, and why did it happen to me today, in New York, and what do I know?

It's a long bus ride back to the apartment. Enough time to be disappointed, a bit angry maybe, and to think. If I had heard the news from Germany during and after the war here from across the ocean, plastered on crazy headlines, I might have seen the horror in black and white. Thought that everybody in Germany must have gone berserk. Only from within can we see it all: the hate, the love, the incredible cruelty and countless kindnesses.

Three weeks till the baby's birth. Irene needs her Mother now and I will leave. I found an apartment to share far from Ali, and in six months, Gernot and Irene will move to Munich. They want a large home so I can live with them if I want to.

56

NEW LOVE SWEETER THAN WINE

I hop onboard the turboprop airliner just before liftoff and get rushed to my seat. They nearly left me behind. Everybody is sitting and seat belted. I am hoping for a quiet, unobtrusive neighbor.

A young man is sitting in the middle seat of my row. He gets up with a quick smile, a short 'hello,' and puts my suitcase in the overhand bin. I get to my window seat and he goes back to looking at a brochure as if I didn't exist. Good! He is not a loquacious man and I won't have to listen to his problems. He is also not overflowing into my seat, and he doesn't smell bad. A perfect person to sit next to me for the next many hours. His hands are huge and wide, not long and elegant like Ali's, and his feet take up his whole floor space. Kind of like Gernot's. He puts down the brochure and picks up a book. As subtle as possible, I turn my eyes to read its title. Darn it! He notices and slides his eyes right into mine. They are twinkling. He caught me.

"It's Hemingway," he says. "A bit demanding for a dirt farmer like me." He still has his twinkle. Darn! I am embarrassed and annoyed. I did hope for a few more words but that's all the crumbs I get. He continues to read for the next two hours. I stare out the window into a solid cloud cover and pout. Yes! I pout over a guy I am not attracted to, who is not my type, and whose head isn't even round. It is strangely square, and his dark blonde hair turns into curls right behind his ears. His big nose sits squat in the middle of his face like a score board. You can't miss it. And every time he turns a page of his book, he licks his finger. When I need the restroom, he gets up for me. Some men make you slide and squeeze over them, but not he, the perfect gentleman. He is tall, over six feet for sure, and strong. He could easily carry me over the doorsill or up a ladder into the hayloft. I am being silly.

The trolleys are bringing our food. My fish has an odor and tastes oily and I scrunch my nose. Yuck!

"I'll trade your fish for dessert," he says. I nod my head and we exchange our food. He takes a bite of my fish, gags and spits it into a tissue.

"I'll trade you back. As an old fisherman, this fish is nasty."

He cuts off a generous piece of his tiny airline steak and puts it on my plate.

I taste the chocolate pudding before handing it back. I would have liked to keep it. He dips his finger in, licks it and gives me back the rest.

"You want it more than I do, right?" His eyes are a nice hazel color.

"Anything with chocolate is good." I ask how he can be both a farmer and a fisherman.

"There are tens of pots with herbs and flowers on my patio and I keep an aquarium in the living room."

"Really? I kissed a guy once. So now I am a whore?"

"A whorible person." The guy makes me laugh. He is the woodsy kind, probably loves to wear dirty boots, and I ask if he likes to hike.

"My favorite. Hiking up the mountains, finding a stream or a cool lake for fishing and skinny dipping – if it gets hot. Nothing like the quiet."

He wants me to shut up and I take out my book 'Rebecca' by Du Maurier.

"A good one," he says approvingly, as he continues his own.

Next thing, I hear a 'plop'. His book dropped. Then there's the weight of his square head leaning into me, a subtle snore, his breath warming my right breast. I am his pillow, soft and drooled upon, and I am falling asleep myself.

"Coffee or tea?" Our heads are almost colliding from the jolt, and he says in a sleepy voice,

"You have a melodious snore, the best I've ever slept with."

"It was your own. You fell asleep and your head is the heaviest I've ever slept with."

"So, we were sleeping together?"

"Keep dreaming." I turn away so he can't see my very cheerful face.

He takes a coffee. I need water to cool off. He is fanning my sex hormones as the perfect kindling for his wicked humor. Then he settles comfortably in with his book while I pretend to read.

. . .

We are close to landing in Iceland. The next plane has engine trouble and we get bussed into a hotel. 'To be back by 9:00 a.m.' we are told. For some reason, and I am seriously not trying, I follow him like a pet. When I don't, he follows me. We end up in the hotel's restaurant at a little table for two. He orders a bottle of wine. We start drinking before the meal comes. After a large glass, gulped down from thirst, I feel weak and drowsy, maybe inebriated since I barely drink wine, and I dig into my chicken leg which seemed to have arrived on its own one leg, I sure didn't order it, and I don't bother using silverware.

"You'll make a good farmer's wife," he comments with his annoying twinkle. Yes, I call it annoying to keep me from what exactly I am not sure. He is not my type. Hell, there is no chemistry between us, no lightning bolt that brings me to my knees. But I like him, really like him, and it's a new feeling of some kind or another. We are comfortably chatting and chewing away, getting to know each other quite well if not a bit lopsided. He looks through me in an almost uncomfortably comfortable way, wants to know about my family and I can't stop talking about my parents, about Gernot and how I found his brother but lost Hartmut. The many years Ulla and I serenaded our neighbor. I even tell him about Luis, my first love and its pain. And just a few words about Ali. I wish I hadn't. It is still a sore spot in my heart. My words are spewing at him like rocks from a volcano. Or like a drunkard.

"I am not used to wine, sorry for my motor mouth."

"I enjoyed it. I promise to use my own limited vocabulary during our six-hour flight tomorrow."

He takes me upstairs to my room, holding me by my elbow so as not to fall flat on my ass, tells me to be ready at 7:00 a.m. for breakfast and leaves me sitting on my bed. Doesn't even try to kiss me. I mean, the guy and I slept together!

. . .

We, whose name I don't even know, are sitting together again in a much larger airplane. It is not full, and he grabbed the seat next to me. My hangover hurts. I barely slept. And I didn't have breakfast. And now his head is slowly falling over again, coming to rest on my shoulder with those soft little snores. It's our last leg of the long trip. A strong leg. For a while I try to dream of him and his legs, but they run away from me. Instead, a large hand slides over me and finds my left breast. No, he is not grabbing it, just resting on it. There is a difference and I refuse to wake up. It might disappear.

"Sorry to wake you. What would you like for lunch?" The trolley people again.

"No fish."

"No fish."

They bring us beef. But the spell is broken, his hand back in his lap. He flashes his best ear to ear smile at me.

"We slept together again! Maybe the third time will finally be comfortable." His twinkle is back. Even a little smirk, but a nice one, not the lecherous kind.

"I don't even know your name."

"Johannes. And you are Sabine. Your name was called twice in New York. You were late." And he grabs my hand to shake it.

"You are neither a farmer nor a fisherman, Johannes. And in some strange way you are worse than any flirt I've ever met. You confuse me."

"I dream about being a farmer or a fisherman but make my living as an engineer. Just got back from an intense week of technology in California. You are my antidote. Thank you."

Antidote, that's what I am, a shot in his arm. I could be his antelope or we could elope.

. . .

"What are you thinking about?"

"You don't want to know! My thoughts jump around in weird ways."

"So do mine. I won't laugh."

"A shot in the arm, an antidote, an antelope ... never mind..."

"grope... elope?...."

Didn't he promise not to laugh? I turn bright red but start laughing right alongside him, and he pats my hand for a while till I take it back.

He is a slow reader and I finish my big book at the same time. The airplane will land soon. We are in our seatbelts, seat in the upright position. Will we see each other again? I don't even know where he lives and already miss him but don't want to ask. I want him to do the asking.

He is checking his calendar. I look over his shoulders, comfortable to do so after sleeping with him twice.

"I could pick you up for lunch next Wednesday."

"Your calendar is full."

"It's full but I got to eat. I'll meet you at 12:00 noon at the café near the main entry of the Law School." He takes an eraser and erases two whole days.

"Are we going to eat for two whole days? And what if I get sick or fall in love on Tuesday?" He is confident neither will happen, and I can't stop smiling, and the butterflies in my belly are wildly flapping their wings, and their long antennas give me quivers.

. . .

At the airport, he stops at a food stand and buys me an apple, three large buttered pretzels, a large bar of Swiss chocolate and a bottle of apple juice for the long train ride home. Then he rushes off to catch his own train. All I get is a tiny hug with lips barely touching my neck.

Wednesday, one week later. I am early and plant myself at a small table with a view at trees and flowering shrubs. He is late. I order mint tea. Heavy steps make me turn around and I see his expectant joyous face. We embrace rather indulgently. Our pulses are racing, and an unbearable longing for him renders me speechless. We did not expect such a hot encounter. He is very quiet but holds my hand across the table.

"I missed you," is all he says. I simply nod my head. We keep looking at each other in our newfound puppy love. Then we order and eat with little talk.

It's been five weeks with as many Wednesday lunches. I've told him about Ali but not about the baby, I just can't, not without crying. Not in a restaurant.

"I need to tell you something. I'd rather be in nature when that happens. How about next Wednesday we meet in a park, I'll bring lunch?"

"How about a picnic in the mountains this Saturday? I'll bring lunch and my brother. We'll have plenty of alone time, he loves to walk ahead, mainly when I tell him to."

. . .

I feel strangely and wildly happy about meeting a part of his family. His name is Josef, a comfortable guy to be with, just like Johannes. They are whole within themselves, a most desirable trait in a person. I never realized that before. We drive deep into the mountains, park and hike up a steep path. There's a beautiful view and an old tree trunk 'with the face of his grandmother,' says Josef. Another hour higher, we get to a lake, sweaty and ready. We strip and jump in and play like little kids, splashing, laughing and scaring the tiny fish.

When we get out, he covers himself and throws me a towel.

"You peeked," I say.

"Only at the bare parts."

We eat our buttered bread, bananas and chocolates, and I thank Josef for being my chaperone.

"Oh no, Johannes begged me to be HIS chaperone."

"Is that true, Johannes?"

"There is a kernel of truth in it." And his twinkle turns me on like a 200 Volt lightbulb.

On the way down, Josef speeds up. He says he loves to run down steep hills. I think he wants us to be alone. It's hard to change my mood, and I say nothing for most of the way down. Then I cry and he holds me, and we find a spot to sit, and I talk. He hears me out to the end.

"I am glad you told me. I sensed some deep sorrow in you besides Ali."

He hugs me for a long time. Then he steps away.

"You know I am falling madly in love with you."

I nod my head, say 'me too,' and instead of kissing we hold hands and run down the hill to the safety of our chaperone.

. . .

The next time we meet, he asks me to his company's annual party as his date and gladly, I accept. Would he mind if I wore one of my outfits from Ali with matching shoes? They make me look glamorous!

"I won't mind," he says. "After all, the woolen socks I wore on our hike were knitted by a girlfriend. If you had only looked at them, you would have noticed the delicate pattern and excellent craftsmanship."

I buy new underwear; for myself, I want to believe, but suddenly realize that it's more like 'just in case.' I like the guy, really truly like him. There is a new happiness in my heart whenever we meet and an emptiness when we don't. Ali is the past. We needed each other while it lasted, a real-life workshop teaching us about ourselves. He saw too much potential in me, while I learned to live up only to my own expectations. I am good enough for me and free to find my own new scent.

The party takes place at a hotel in Munich. I get introduced to about a hundred people, in fact, to all of them. They seem delighted to meet me, and he seems well liked.

There is a stage in the large room. Johannes says he'll be right back, then hops onto the stage and the hall becomes quiet. He gives a speech, thanking the audience for their hard work, promises a bonus since the trip to California was a success.

"In more ways than one," he says, looking right at me.

After a tasty meal and some other short speeches, we dance. He is an excellent dancer, knows how to move and swirl me around, and we don't miss a dance.

. . .

When the light dims, the music slows, bodies touch, we hold still, and time holds still with us. My nose buries into his neck. I taste his sweat and am suddenly drawn into this man's magnetic field, feel at home, truly at home, and tears start running down my cheeks, just a few, then torrents of them, followed by uncontrollable sobbing. He holds me tight, both arms around me, and all I want is to stand still for the rest of my life, leaning into him. I cry for all the sadnesses in my life, for the love I had with Ali, and mostly for my baby boy, for what should have been, for a dream that was dreamt and woken up from, and for what is happening right now. All my life's sorrows and ecstasies pour out in a gush of salty water and a last squeeze of the tears for Ali.

He leads me outside where we sit down on a bench behind a plant. And he kisses me. I cry some more, we kiss again, I cry again, enough for the plant that is in dire need of water.

"Let's get a room," he says, after more kissing, "don't worry, just to talk." I nod my head, not worried but wanting. Wanting him forever. He gets a room and we go up. We still don't know what happened, but we barely have time to close the door, that's how hungry we are for our bodies to touch and melt.

Sexy underwear is largely overrated. I might as well have worn my pink poodle love killers with the black spider over the butt crack.

EPILOGUE

Petaluma, California

The double swing I am sitting in is home to huge spider webs, showing off their diamond sparkled silk glorified by the sprinkler's watering. The wonder of paradise surrounds me. An abundance of flowers and trees, gardens for food, myriads of different insects, and we all work and feast together, yes, even on each other, in harmony. Eat or be eaten, but gently and gratefully.

How truly fortunate my life has been. Where normal people saw rain, I saw mostly the sunny side, even during the difficult years of hunger and cold. There were always arms around me, loving arms and strong arms instilling a sense of my own strength. It helped me venture into the world with ease and . When Mother began to take me to operas and concerts, and

Father and I became regular patrons and passionate applauders at our small local theatre, my world gained a new richness of beauty and possibilities.

Much later, my dream from 1952 at the beach in France came true. I live under blue skies, palm trees and near the ocean. The only change is the maturing of mens' tiny bathing trunks into a Victorian aged size, hiding any outline of male belly, butt or balls.

I am now 76 years of age and feel my little veined legs sprint towards the end goal. They still run well but I would like to slow them down a bit. 'Let's not hit the goal post yet' I yell, naively trying to buy time. Of course, I can't, but time itself took me by the hand to reminisce and write down my life for you, my kids, grandkids, great grandkids, etc. It is done now, written and not of much use.

However, when you are old and look back at your life, you might enjoy my stories from an ancient time that connect you to a large part of your family dating back into the eighteen-hundreds. May it help you understand my time of life, my quirks, idiosyncrasies or plain idiocies. This story includes you now in its large web. Think about that, my lovely little critters.

There goes Johannes, my beloved husband, with hungry steps towards the house. He has been most supportive of my newfangled hobby of putting so many words together. I better run before he destroys my kitchen.

. . .

It has been an amazing life, filled with everything I could have dreamed of. I found the perfect friend, lover and husband who is always there but lets me be. And my happiness is now, right around us, with kids to be proud of and thankful for, and grand-kids that show their joy and love with enough noise to prove it. To Life! Chaim! Prost!

ALSO BY BEATE DAYEM STAMNESS

The Butcher's Daughter

A Novel of Abuse and Redemption

ABOUT THE AUTHOR

Beate Dayem Stamness lives with her husband in Petaluma, California, where they garden and play at being good grandparents.

www.ingramcontent.com/pod-product-compliance
Lightning Source LLC
Chambersburg PA
CBHW030118260626
47156CB00008B/2703